#13.5

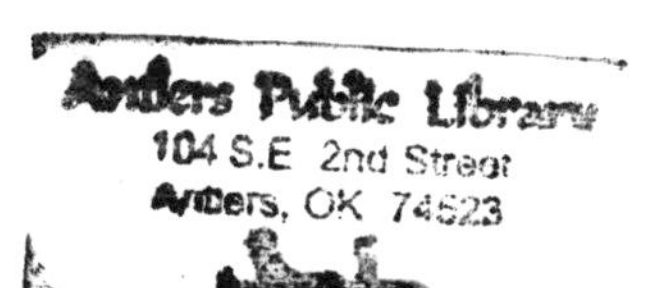
Antlers Public Library
104 S.E 2nd Street
Antlers, OK 74523

Riptide Publishing
PO Box 1537
Burnsville, NC 28714
www.riptidepublishing.com

Cover art: Jay Aheer, jayscoversbydesign.com
Editor: Sarah Frantz Lyons
Layout: L.C. Chase, lcchase.com/design.htm

ISBN: 978-1-62649-309-4

First edition
September, 2015

Also available in ebook:
ISBN: 978-1-62649-308-7

BASE INSTINCTS

A Demonica Story

For the rule-breakers. Life, like imagination, has no limits, so find the loopholes and write your story the way you want it to go.

TABLE OF CONTENTS

GLOSSARY

The Aegis—Society of human warriors dedicated to protecting the world from evil. Recent dissension among its ranks reduced its numbers and sent the Aegis in a new direction.

Fallen Angel—Believed to be evil by most humans, fallen angels can be grouped into two categories: True Fallen and Unfallen. Unfallen angels have been cast from Heaven and are earthbound, living a life in which they are neither truly good nor truly evil. In this state, they can, rarely, earn their way back into Heaven. Or they can choose to enter Sheoul, the demon realm, in order to complete their fall and become True Fallens, taking their places as demons at Satan's side.

Harrowgate—Vertical portals, invisible to humans, that demons use to travel between locations on Earth and Sheoul. A very few beings can summon their own personal Harrowgates.

S'genesis—Final maturation cycle for a Seminus demon. Occurs at one hundred years of age. A post *s'genesis* male is capable of procreation and possesses the ability to shapeshift into the male of nearly any similar-sized demon species.

Sheoul—Demon realm. Located on its own plane deep in the bowels of the Earth, accessible to most only by Harrowgates and hellmouths.

Sheoulic—Universal demon language spoken by all, although many species also speak their own language.

Ter'taceo—Demons who can pass as human, either because their species is naturally human in appearance, or because they can shapeshift into human form.

Ufelskala—A scoring system for demons, based on their degree of evil. All supernatural creatures and evil humans can be categorized into the five Tiers, with the Fifth Tier comprising of the worst of the wicked.

Classification of Demons, as listed by Baradoc, Umber demon, using the demon breed Seminus as an example:

Kingdom: Animalia
Class: Demon
Family: Sexual Demon
Genus: Terrestrial
Species: Incubus
Breed: Seminus

CHAPTER ONE

According to the news, the weather system bearing down on Damon Slake was a proven killer.

But then, Slake was also a killer, and he could guaran-damn-tee that he was far more lethal than any thunderstorm.

Rain and hail pelted him as he stood outside one of several secret entrances to Thirst, a vampire nightclub that operated in the shadows of a human goth hangout called The Velvet Chain. Like most upscale vamp clubs, this one catered to all otherworldly beings, as well as humans who were willing to give themselves up as a snack for those who fed on blood. And, as one of the busiest high-end establishments, this place even had a medical clinic. Reputation was everything, and no club owner wanted to deal with a bunch of human deaths from overfeeding, or demon deaths from a drunken bar fight.

Which was smart, especially now that the recent near-apocalypse had revealed the demon world to humans, causing tension, fear, and chaos. They were in all-out extermination mode, while demons were dealing with some sort of political shakeup in Sheoul, the realm many people called Hell. Slake had no idea what was going on in Sheoul, and frankly, he didn't care. He had a job to do, and he always completed his missions.

His latest prey had been cunning, maybe his most clever adversary yet, but he'd finally tracked her here. The wily succubus had covered her tracks well, but Slake had a knack for ferreting out secrets, and as good as Fayle was at hiding, Slake was better at finding.

Lightning flashed like some sort of horror-movie foreshadowing as he entered the dimly lit club through a doorway only supernatural creatures could see. Instantly, the blare of rock music, the stench of sweating, dancing people, and the electric, sensual energy of sin assailed him. If he hadn't been on the job, he'd revel in the club scene and be scoping out potential partners to take home for the night.

Partners like that sexy-as-hell medic propped against the wall near the first aid station, his gaze sweeping the crowd with the hard-core intensity of a battle-wise soldier in enemy territory. Even from across the room, Slake could see the readiness for anything in the subtle tautness of his body.

And what a body it was. His black uniform was stretched tight across his shoulders and abs, the rolled sleeves revealing thickly muscled arms made to pin his partner to a mattress.

Slake had no idea if the dude was into males, females, or both, but the guy practically oozed confidence and sex. The medic folded his arms over his broad chest, giving Slake a prime view of a sleeve of tattoos winding from his fingers to his biceps, where they disappeared beneath his uniform and then reappeared at the top of his collar. The pattern ended just below his jaw, and Slake decided he'd need to get a closer look, because damn, he loved tats.

And maybe getting in closer would help him figure out what species—or breed—of demon the guy was. He was definitely a demon; Slake's ability to distinguish a blue human aura from an orangey-red demon one made that clear. Not that Slake was picky when it came to bed mates, but he drew the line at fucking any species of demon that rated a five on the Ufelskala scale of evil. Fours were bad enough, but with a five, you never knew whether or not your partner was going to kill you after you came.

Or *before* you came, for that matter.

A scuffle erupted out near the bathrooms, drawing his attention away from the medic, but bouncers broke it up before too much blood spilled. No doubt the fight would be just one of many tonight, but that wasn't Slake's concern. He strode through the club, his eyes peeled for his target. There were approximately a million and a half females milling about, but none resembled the petite, black-haired Asian in the picture he'd been given two months ago by his boss at Dire & Dyre, the law firm that employed him as an Acquirer. Yup, if a client wanted something or someone, Slake was the one sent to acquire it.

Except this job was different. This job would determine the course of the rest of Slake's life.

And the rest of his *after*life.

But hey, as his boss pointed out, it was *only* his *soul* on the line.

The jackass.

He spied an empty booth near an exit to the sewers and made a beeline to it, growling at a burly green-skinned demon who tried to slip into the seat ahead of him. The demon cursed, but one look at Slake's arsenal of weapons peeking out from beneath his leather jacket gave the guy second thoughts. Probably third thoughts too.

A waiter brought Slake a double whiskey, neat, and he settled in, hoping his prey would show her pretty face. In the meantime, though, he didn't see any harm in checking out the medic at the rear of the club a little more.

That male was something special. Even his coloring was perfect. Not too tan, but not pale. And given the guy's reddish hair, shorter in the back than in the front, Slake would bet that close up, he'd have some freckles waiting for the caress of a tongue.

Slake's mouth watered at the thought, and he had to shift to make a little more room in his leathers. But he didn't let his lust distract him from his mission. Not when success meant freedom . . . and failure meant kissing his soul good-bye forever.

He downed half his drink and reached for his cell phone just as the thing vibrated in his coat pocket. The name that flashed on the text screen with a curt, *You there?* was exactly who he'd been wanting to hear from for days. Hoping for good news from his favorite underworld spy, he tapped out a message.

Hey, Atrox, it's about time. Tell me you have an update on our prize.

He waited an unbearably long time for the reply. Atrox's fat fingers and long claws weren't exactly compatible with touchscreen keyboards. The reptilian demon had to use his knuckles to type, which Slake had found funny . . . until lizard boy had used those knuckles to knock Slake on his ass.

Finally, the phone beeped with Atrox's incoming text. *Got a lead. One of the dudes I grilled last night is a regular at Thirst. Said he's seen the succubus several times in the company of a male with red hair and a sleeve of tats on his right arm.*

Red hair and a sleeve of tats. Slake looked up at the hot medic and grinned.

This assignment had just gotten interesting.

The blood was flowing freely tonight.

Sure, the same could be said of any night at Thirst, but between the vampires feeding from the humans and the fights breaking out between all species as the moon hovered on the verge of becoming full, Raze had been one busy, exhausted medic. He'd been on duty for nine hours with only one slow period, and as he watched a heated argument break out at the bar, he knew it was time to gear up for another patch job.

Too bad, too, because that dark-haired male sitting alone in the far corner intrigued him. Intrigued him enough that for the first time in years, Raze was tempted to give in to a desire he rarely indulged in.

The argument escalated into physical violence, swelling from the original three instigators to eight, no, ten guys. One of the bartenders, a lion shifter named Lexi, shouted for the bouncers, who were already on the way. They started pulling people apart, but it took the club owner, Nate, and the manager, Marsden, both vampires, wading into the fray and tossing the fighters aside like rag dolls to break it up.

As Raze gloved up in preparation for treating injuries, most of the participants slunk away like beaten dogs to lick their wounds, but one hairy, horned dude got the boot out the side door. Another, his hand pressed against a gushing wound in this thigh, was dragged, cursing and growling, into the clinic and plopped onto the exam table.

Marsden and Lexi both gave Raze a look of sympathy and got the hell out of there before Raze could recruit them to help.

"Thanks, guys," Raze shouted after them. "Next time you cut yourself while you're slicing up limes, don't come crying to me."

Lexi cast him a saucy grin from over her shoulder while flipping him the bird with a freshly bandaged middle finger. Mars did the same, minus the saucy grin and bandage.

Laughing, he turned to his patient, who, if his sneer was any indication, didn't have the same sense of humor as Mars and Lexi.

Damn it, Raze shouldn't have answered the phone when Thirst's number popped up on his caller ID this morning. This was supposed to have been his day off from both the club and Underworld General, not that he'd had any exciting plans. There weren't even any good new movies out.

The patient bared his teeth at Raze, his slightly elongated fangs indicating that the dude wasn't human. From the musky stench of him, Raze was going to guess he was some sort of animal shifter or were-creature, but given the approach of the full moon and its effects on weres, Raze was going to go with the latter.

"What's your name?" Raze asked as he pulled the tray of first aid equipment toward him.

"Bite me."

Oh yeah, this was going to be a good time. "Okay, Bite Me, what species are you?"

Bite Me narrowed his eyes. "Why the fuck does it matter? You gonna treat me different if I'm something you don't like?"

Apparently, Bite Me was not only a mean drunk, he was one of those fun people who made everything about themselves and their personal views. "It's important because every species and breed is unique, and each one has different medical needs and reactions to treatment." Bite Me didn't seem to be convinced, so Raze elaborated. "Dogs can take aspirin, but it's toxic to cats. Oni demons will burst into flame if exposed to hydrogen peroxide, but it affects Sora demons the way alcohol affects humans." He gestured to a suture kit on the equipment tray. "Some species can't tolerate my healing power and need more traditional methods to close wounds. So stop being a prick and tell me what you are."

Hatred rolled off Bite Me's body as he locked gazes with Raze in a bold challenge. "Guess."

"Well," Raze drawled, "given your overdeveloped canines, foul stench, and sparkling personality, I'd say you're a werewolf."

"It's *warg*, you Seminus scum," the guy growled.

Raze's hand jerked in surprise, not at the word—"warg" was what werewolves preferred to be called—but at the fact that the guy knew what a Seminus demon was. He kept his expression neutral, unwilling to let this unibrowed meathead know he'd struck a nerve.

"Congratulations," he said flatly. "You have correctly identified an extremely rare breed of sex demon."

The guy's upper lip curled. "That's because I've killed two of you bastards."

Raze inhaled deeply, willing himself to stay calm. People killing Seminus demons happened too often, and unfortunately, much of it was deserved. Raze didn't even want to think about how, if he didn't bond with a female by the time he turned a hundred, he'd go through the second of two maturation processes: gaining fertility, a facial marking, and an unholy, uncontrollable need for sex. In fifty short years, he'd become a beast whose primary instinct was to reproduce, and any female within dick's reach would be a target . . . willing or not.

Males of all species killed mature Sems on sight, which Raze figured was pretty understandable. Especially given that all offspring from a Seminus mating were born male Seminus demons—no matter what species the mother was. Raze's own mother had been some sort of cave-dweller demon, but DNA tests performed at Underworld General hadn't been able to identify the exact species, let alone the breed.

"Well, good for you," Raze said, as he not-so-gently slapped his hand over the werewolf's wound and activated his healing power. Stinging energy flowed through the markings on his arm, lighting them up like molten iron. In his mind, he saw the torn vessels, veins, and tissue in the wound begin to knit together. "Not everyone can go up against a Sem and survive. So . . . you gonna tell me your name? Or would you rather I keep calling you Bite Me? Because I'm fine with that."

"I'm Heath, you demon parasite."

"Parasite? That's a little harsh. And unoriginal." Raze sent another wave of power into Heath's leg—but not to heal. This one was made of pain. Heath yelped, and Raze smiled. "Don't fuck with the guy who is patching you up, asshole. I can just as easily kill you as heal you, and my boss is good at disposing of bodies. Keep that in mind."

Heath leaned forward, teeth bared, canines elongating. "I'd rather die than let a filthy *demon* heal me."

"Fine with m—"

In a sudden burst of fury, the bastard snared Raze by the throat and hauled him off his feet. Dude was strong, but then, werewolves were known for their strength. And their bad breath.

The werewolf stood, lifting Raze with him, his fingers squeezing Raze's windpipe in a bruising hold. "One of you fucks stole my woman."

There was nothing more cliché than a thick-skulled werewolf vowing revenge against an entire species because he'd been humiliated.

Raze would have said as much, but merely breathing took effort—talking was out of the question. He glanced over Heath's shoulder and saw Marsden moving in to help, his broad, tall form shoving through the crowd like a bulldozer. Raze met his gaze, gave him the *Back off, I've got this* blink, and in a quick surge, he powered up his healing gift and jammed his fingers against Heath's temple. Instantly, the power Raze normally used to heal ripped skin and flesh apart at a cellular level.

The werewolf shouted in agony and dropped Raze to the ground. Spinning, Raze clamped his hand around the back of Heath's neck and frog-marched the idiot through the rear of the club toward the back door. Marsden trailed behind like a shadow, content to let Raze handle his own messes, but when Mars slipped into the security office, Raze knew he'd be watching everything through the state-of-the-art surveillance system.

Raze shoved open the door and gave the camera overhead a smirk as he shoved Heath outside. The meathead took an awkward swing the moment they stepped out into the pouring rain, and yup, Raze's patience meter had pegged out. With a hard shove, he sent the guy stumbling through the puddles in the alley.

"You're banished, asshole," Raze growled.

"Fuck you." Clutching his head in one hand, Heath wheeled around and slammed his fist into Raze's jaw.

Raze hit the closed door in a crunch of spine, and *damn* that hurt. Pain radiated across his back and through his rib cage with such force that even taking a breath stung. Lightning flashed as the werewolf came at him again, but Raze ducked and spun, barely avoiding a blow that would have broken a lot of bones in his face.

Son of a bitch. This fucker needed to be put down like the rabid dog he was. Raze had never liked werewolves, but this one was a special kind of stupid, stubborn jackass.

With a roar, Raze charged the guy, nailing him in the gut with his shoulder. Heath *oofed* and stumbled backward, but he managed to bring down his fist like a hammer on the back of Raze's neck. Raze hit the wet pavement in a crack of kneecaps, his ears ringing and his eyes blurring. He thought he heard a high-pitched whine followed by another hefty *oof*, and when his vision cleared, he caught an eyeful of Heath the Dick, his mouth smashed in a bloody mess, spitting blood, teeth, and . . . a marble?

Before the guy could recover from the injury that had shattered his grill, Raze readied his power and leaped to his feet. Thunder ripped through the air as he threw a right hook that laid the werewolf out hard, putting him facedown and unmoving on the pavement.

He shook out his fist, knowing he'd feel that punch in his knuckles later. Then, out of the corner of his eye . . . movement. Slowly, he shifted his body around, and there in the shadows, casually leaning against the brick wall of the building across the alley, was the leather-clad male who'd been eyeing him inside.

And in his hand, bouncing in his palm, was a small, glowing ball the size of a marble . . . just like the one the werewolf had spit out. Whatever it was, it was one hell of a weapon. But as Raze took in the stranger, whose dark eyes were gleaming with an eerie silver light, the hairs on the back of his neck stood up, and he realized that as dangerous as the little glowing projectile was, its owner was far, far more lethal.

CHAPTER TWO

If Slake hadn't been turned on before, watching the medic take down the werewolf had given him a raging hard-on. Whatever species the medic was, he had a killer power in that right arm, and even now, his tats were glowing, pulsing with residual energy.

Slake rolled the smooth, ice-cold *sinisphere* between his fingers before pocketing it and pushing away from the side of the building. "Nice, man. You laid that dude *out*."

The medic gestured at the unconscious werewolf. "Wasn't me who had him spitting teeth."

Slake shrugged. "I have fun toys."

The medic muttered something that sounded like, "I'll bet you do."

Slake grinned. He really did have some great playthings, and some of them weren't even for killing or maiming. "I'm Slake."

"Raze." Raze bent over the werewolf, allowing for a tantalizing view of his ass wrapped like a gift in those perfect-fitting black BDU-style pants. Slake watched as he grabbed the unconscious idiot by the ankles and dragged him toward the Harrowgate Slake had used to get here. The gate, invisible to human eyes, had been set into the brick wall, its archway shimmering in invitation. Raze disappeared inside with the werewolf and then leaped back out as the gate closed.

"Where'd you send him?"

"Underworld General. Let them deal with the asshole."

Slake snorted. "You're nicer than I am. I'd have left him here for the vultures."

"New York doesn't have a big vulture population." Raze dug something out of his pocket, unwrapped it, and popped it into his mouth. "But it does have a big werewolf problem."

As far as Slake was concerned, the *world* had a big werewolf problem. Dumb mutts. They didn't even get along with members of their own species. "I hear you. We got something in common."

There was a subtle stiffening in the set of Raze's shoulders that lasted only a second before he started moving toward the door of the club. "Didn't know we were looking for shit to bond over."

So the game was hard-to-get. Slake could play that way. For a time, at least. The medic had given him enough looks for Slake to sense the guy's taste for males, but if Raze was, indeed, the guy Atrox said had been hanging out with Fayle, things might get a little complicated.

Or maybe they could be real damned simple. Fuck the guy, take the girl, save a soul.

His soul.

"I didn't say anything about bonding." Slake moved toward Raze. Slowly. Purposefully. "But I wouldn't mind getting to know you. Got a girlfriend?"

Raze came to a halt a couple of feet from the entrance. "No."

"Boyfriend?"

Raze swung around, his green eyes darkening. "You have no idea what I am, do you?"

"Should I?" Slake advanced on him, enjoying how Raze's body tensed and his breaths became more rapid. "Are you . . . dangerous? Aside from that crazy shit you do with your tats."

One corner of Raze's mouth tipped up in a half smile. "I'm only dangerous if you piss me off."

"What if I *get* you off?"

Raze barked out a laugh. "Man, what do you want from me?"

Slake got close, invading the other male's personal space. The guy would either stand his ground or back off, and either one would speak volumes about him.

Tension filled the narrow gap between them, pulsing like a heartbeat. Raze was taller than Slake's six three by maybe half an inch, but Slake outweighed him by a good twenty-five pounds, and as they stood there taking each other's measure, he had to admire that Raze didn't back down. Most dudes who went toe-to-toe with him did so out of macho arrogance, but the calculation and intelligence flashing in Raze's eyes said he was holding his ground for a different reason.

Raze was attracted to him.

But he was suspicious. Which was smart.

"What do I want from you?" Slake reached out, brushed a finger over Raze's jugular, once again watching. Gauging. And hoping. "I want to buy you a drink. Is that too much to ask?"

"I don't drink."

"Why not?" Alcohol was poison to some species, while in others, there was no effect at all, no matter how much they ingested. Anyone else who didn't drink was just weird in Slake's opinion.

Raze's hand snapped up to grab Slake's wrist in a hold that walked the line between pain and . . . well, not pain. But it felt good to be touched. Too good.

"Alcohol can't make me drunk, but it does make me want what I can't have."

"And what," he said softly, "is that?"

Releasing him with an angry shove, Raze pivoted smoothly toward the club. Oh hell no. Slake wasn't done with the medic. Raze was probably associated with the female Slake was looking for, and even if he wasn't . . . well, there was just something about the guy that intrigued him. Besides, Slake had never been one to give up easily. He'd have been dead a long time ago.

With a low growl, Slake snagged Raze's shoulder and spun him back around. Surprise and anger flashed in the medic's expression, and in that moment of startled disbelief, Slake took advantage like the predator he was, pressing his body against Raze's as he brought their mouths together.

Instant, sizzling lust shot through Slake, sparking nerve endings to life and shocking his heart into an erratic rhythm. But low on his back, the scar from an ancient stab wound began to throb, a reminder to never surrender entirely, not even to a sultry kiss that could potentially lead to more. He needed to keep his mind focused, clear, and aware of everything going on around him. Like the cool breeze that rattled the trash on the ground and smelled like rain. Or the drip of water from the downspout a few yards away. And the sound of honking horns and squealing tires from the street traffic.

No one and nothing would ever sneak up on him again.

Hungrily, he fisted Raze's hair and increased the pressure on his mouth. Raze's lips were firm, unyielding, and tasted of the sweet caramel candy he'd eaten a moment ago. Decadence, Slake thought, as he swept his tongue along the seam of Raze's mouth, urging him to open. Raze stubbornly clenched his teeth and snarled softly, but Slake persisted with lingering, sensual licks. Just when he thought he'd lost the battle, Raze's tongue clashed with his in a hot, wet struggle for dominance.

One strong hand cupped the back of Slake's head and another slid around his waist to draw him even tighter against Raze. The press of Raze's erection into his made Slake groan as a fresh wave of lust rolled over him, dulling the edges of the situational awareness he prided himself on maintaining.

Shit. It was time to put the brakes on—

"Asshole." Raze jerked away and stepped back. He was breathing heavy, his lips swollen and glistening, and Slake wondered if he looked as punch-drunk as Raze did. "There are at least a dozen guys inside who would let you blow them on top of the freaking bar with an audience if you wanted. So why me?"

Because you might be the key to locating the female I'm after. The thought flew through Slake's brain, but on its heels was something unexpected. Startling.

"Because something about you makes me want to throw caution to the wind, and I never do that."

"Why not?"

Slake shrugged. "Letting down your guard gets you dead."

One ginger eyebrow cocked, but the wariness in Raze's eyes never lessened. "You must live a dangerous life."

Slake shrugged again. "You know what they say. You feel the most alive when death is on your doorstep."

"Death, huh?" Raze laughed, a deep, throaty sound that went straight to Slake's groin. "You have no idea."

"Yeah? Then why don't you educate me?"

"No need." Raze threw open the door to the club. "You're a dick, so I have no doubt that death will come for you soon enough."

With that, Raze disappeared, likely not even realizing how right he probably was.

Raze practically ran through the club, hitting the medic office in record time. Vladlena, the owner's shifter mate and a coworker at Underworld General, had arrived for her shift, so he gave her a quick status update and darted out the back of the club and into a narrow alley separating Thirst from the apartments across the way. Quickly, he yanked open the dented metal door and took the stairs to the third floor.

The stairs were old, wooden, and he swore they wobbled under every step. It wasn't until he slammed into his place and sagged against the door that he realized the stairs were fine. *He* was shaking.

What. The. Fuck.

His mind kept replaying the alley scene in vivid detail, and with every passing second, his body heated more, his breathing grew more rapid, and his cock throbbed harder. He knew very well what arousal was, but this . . . this was different than anything he'd ever experienced. This wasn't need. It was *want*, and on a level he couldn't have comprehended before now.

As he sucked in panting breaths, he heard soft footfalls. Fayle. Shit. Schooling his expression, he pushed away from the door, but the look on the succubus's ageless face told him she already knew what was going on.

"You aren't due for a release for another four hours," she said. "Which means *some male* got you all worked up."

Gods, she was so freaking possessive. And the really fucked-up thing about it was that she didn't even want Raze. At least, not for a relationship. They'd been together for nearly thirty years in a symbiotic partnership that operated on mutual respect and friendship, but there was no intimacy, no touching, no kissing, not since the day they'd met. There were no romantic feelings between them at all. That was fine with Raze, and it was exactly what he wanted from her, but sometimes the way she controlled and coveted the things she considered to be hers got frustrating.

"I thought you were out for the day," he said, hoping the residual lust in his voice wasn't as obvious to her as it was to him, but that was wishful thinking, and deep down, he knew it.

Fayle stood on the bright-yellow rug in the living room, her arms crossed under breasts that every straight man ogled no matter what she was wearing. "I went out to buy another suitcase. Now I'm packing."

Raze held back a groan. Not this again. "Fayle, we're not moving."

One dark eyebrow cocked and her mouth tightened into a stubborn line as she stared at him. He met her silence with a refusal to engage further, moving to the fridge for a soda instead. As he popped the top off a bottle of root beer, he heard her curse softly. A moment later, she was in front of him in the kitchen, her fingers reaching for the fly of his pants.

"Let me take care of you."

He stepped back. "I'm fine."

She huffed. "You aren't fine. You're pale and sweating."

"I haven't hit the point of no return." He skirted around her to head toward the living room. "This will pass."

Fayle followed. "How far did you get with him?"

Not far at all, which was why this sucked so much. Raze was way more turned on than he should be. "Far enough, apparently."

Knowing he couldn't escape her, he halted at the threshold to the living room, which Fayle had decorated in glaringly bright colors. She hated subdued, natural tones, which meant that everything around her looked like a box of crayons had exploded.

She came around in front of him and shoved her straight black bangs away from her eyes. "Why didn't you bring him up here?"

"I already told you. I thought you were gone." As a Seminus demon, he needed sex or he would die, but he couldn't get off with males, which meant that if he wanted to have sex with one, he needed a female to be present. Fayle had accommodated Raze's desire for males on occasion, but she made life hell for him for months afterward and for the most part, he'd resigned himself to the fact that he couldn't have what he wanted. That he could never have a relationship with a male, even for casual sex.

"Well, now I'm back." She gestured to her bedroom. "Maybe you can help me pack my things, and then we can box up yours."

Sighing, Raze sank down on the couch and threw his feet up on the coffee table. "I'm tired of moving, Fayle. I finally have a job I like. Friends. A life. I'm happy."

Well, mostly. There was a hole inside he couldn't fill with work. Or friends. Or sex. And every time he felt a glimmer of attraction for a male, the hole got bigger. Even now, after those few minutes with Slake, it was as if the hole had become a bottomless pit, magnifying and echoing his loneliness.

Fayle made a sound of long-suffering impatience. "You know my species is nomadic. I'm going crazy. We've already been here for a year longer than I wanted to be. We need to go. I was thinking . . . Tokyo. Or Manila. We've never lived in Manila. I hear there's a pretty good sex scene happening there."

As a succubus who fed on the sexual energy of those engaging nearby, Fayle liked densely populated areas. Naturally, Raze preferred the exact opposite.

"I said no."

A blast of anger hit him in a psychic wave that made his brain hurt. Fayle never had learned to control her emotional outbursts. "Maybe I'll go without you."

She'd made that threat before—several times, in fact. Eventually, his gratitude for the fact that she'd saved his life by helping him through his sexual transition won out and he'd always given in, even though he was pretty sure she wasn't serious. This time, though, the anger accompanying her words was different. More intense. Maybe she wasn't bluffing.

And maybe he wasn't, either.

He snared the remote and turned on TV. Ooh, maybe Dr. Phil could help. Ten seconds later, he realized Dr. Phil could only help if Raze's problem was a controlling mother-in-law and a drug-addicted kid.

"Well?" Fayle tapped her foot on the concrete floor. "Do I have to go by myself?"

"Do what you have to do."

She moved to stand in front of the TV, blocking Dr. Phil and the guest's heroine-addled douche of a son.

"How dare you?" she snapped. "After I saved your life? After I spent the last thirty years giving you what you need to stay alive?"

"I'm grateful, Fayle." Meeting her gaze, he leaned forward, hoping she'd believe his sincerity. "You know that." He'd only said as much a zillion times. "But I can get sex from other females. I've never forced you to stay with me."

He had to admit, though, that having a permanent partner made his life a lot easier. Most unmated Seminus demons had to scrounge up a partner every few hours. Fayle had made herself available to Raze anytime he needed her since he'd turned twenty and she'd helped him through his first stage of maturation, when he could have died without her.

"You are such a bastard," she snapped. "I don't believe you're grateful."

He blew out a long, frustrated breath. They had this argument more often than any other. If he didn't tell her constantly that he was grateful for everything she'd done, she threw godawful temper tantrums.

"I thank you every single day," he said.

"Words." She waved her hand in dismissal. "I want action. Move with me."

"See, that's the problem." He looked down at the floor between his spread legs and shook his head. "I'd be more than happy to move, but that's not what you want. You want me to quit my jobs too."

"To prevent anyone from tracking us. You know how much I'm risking by being with you."

He lifted his gaze sharply, unable to believe she just said that. "Actually, no, I don't. Every time I ask, you shut down or change the subject. So how about, after thirty fucking years of being together, you tell me what will happen if your people find you?"

Her chin came up and the stubborn came out. "It's private."

Standing, he slammed the bottle of root beer on the coffee table, splashing liquid onto the shiny surface. "Everything is private with you. I don't know anything about your species. I don't know anything about your family or your life before we got together. So maybe it's about time you stopped expecting me to roll over every time you tell me to, just because you *saved my life*."

Fury turned her face red. "You . . . you . . ."

"Yeah, yeah, I'm a bastard. A bastard who's supported you financially and emotionally for the last three decades. I even do all the cooking. You wander around sucking up sexual energy from people, and sometimes you pick up a few things at the grocery store. So stop acting like I deny you anything."

The muscles in her jaw leaped angrily as she ground her molars. "I've saved your life more than once," she bit out. "You always seem to forget that. And I keep you alive every day." She cast his groin a pointed glance and then shot him a wicked smile that made his balls shrivel. "But tonight, I think I'll let you be reminded of how much you need me."

With that, she stormed off to her bedroom. His cock throbbed, as if it knew what had just happened. He'd need sex in about four hours or pain would set in. Which meant Fayle would wait to come to him until he was desperate enough to beg.

Oh, sure, he could find himself another female fairly quickly. Thirst was crawling with horny demons, vampires, and humans who would respond to the pheromones his body would be throwing out like a drug. But he didn't want to screw strange females. Hell, he didn't even want Fayle, but at least with her, there was no pretense, no messy seduction, no awkward postcoital conversation.

Unfortunately, what he wanted was something he couldn't have.

And for some reason, Slake's face popped into his head, the poster boy for Can't Have.

His cock throbbed again.

The fucker.

CHAPTER THREE

The Big Boss's office at Dire & Dyre Hong Kong was, to the untrained eye, plush, extravagant, and elegant. Slake doubted a single speck of dust would dare to settle on any of the polished surfaces.

But to those who knew better, the office was a sinister dungeon filled with lethal traps and ensorcelled relics that could melt eyeballs, hypnotize the unsuspecting, or boil a person's blood in their veins.

That Ming vase on the bookshelf across from where Slake was sitting? Sure, it was priceless, but it also contained the ashes of a Charnel Apostle that, if sprinkled in the flame of the black candle next to it, would drain a hundred years off the life of the nearest demon.

The painting of the cherubic baby angel with the sweet smile on the wall behind the Big Boss? Yeah, with a whispered command, the angel's eyes would light up with heat that steamed the skin off its intended victim.

Slake was always pretty uneasy in the room.

Not, of course, that he showed any sign of being nervous. Nope. In fact, he made a point of casually lounging in the uncomfortable wooden chair across from the Big Boss. Frank Dire, humans called him—humans who were clueless about the fact that he was *ter'taceo*, a demon in a human suit. To his inner circle, he was Dyre, and he was as evil as anyone Slake had ever known.

He was, all by himself, Dire & Dyre. He was Dire *and* Dyre, and when human clients demanded meetings with both "partners," he had the ability to replicate himself for short periods of time, but only after sacrificing an innocent. The dude was a definite five on the Ufelskala scale of evil.

"So." From across the polished mahogany desk the size of a freaking pool table, Dyre stared at Slake, his dark irises ringed by glowing scarlet. The demon inside had come out to play today. Not a good sign. "You haven't completed your assignment."

"I'm close." Slake eased back in the chair even more and crossed his booted feet at the ankles, the very picture of *everything's cool.* "I've tracked her to a vampire club in New York. She's been seen in the company of a certain male."

The neutral expression on Dyre's deceptively handsome face didn't change. "Her species is parasitic. Did she attach herself to that male?"

"Unclear. But I'm working on finding out." If she had, it was possible that Raze would sense if she were in trouble. And a kidnapping probably counted as trouble.

Dyre picked up a gold pen and began flipping it between his fingers. Slake tensed. The guy was the most dangerous when he appeared the most casual. "The client has been very patient."

Slake slid a glance at the angel painting. No melty eyes. So far, so good. "The client didn't provide a lot to go on."

"You've never needed a lot to go on," Dyre countered. "You're one of Dire & Dyre's best hunters. So why is it taking you so long to track down one parasitic succubus?"

Gods, he was impatient. "It's only been a month—"

"You have one week to complete your assignment."

Slake shot out of his chair. "One . . . week? That's bullshit! I was supposed to have until the end of next month."

"The clients moved up the timeline."

Son of a bitch. "Why?"

"That's their business."

"Yeah, well my *soul* is my business, and it's affected by this new deadline."

Dyre's lips peeled back to reveal his shiny white teeth and big-ass fangs. "Your soul is also *my* business."

As if Slake needed the reminder that Dire & Dyre didn't exist just to make a lot of money. It existed to collect souls too, and Slake's would become another of the law firm's assets if he failed to bring in Fayle before the deadline.

Slake ground his molars so hard his jaw ached. "Yes, sir."

Dyre smiled. "Good. Now that we're in agreement, go complete your assignment."

That had been way too easy, and with so much on the line, Slake couldn't pass up an opportunity to dig a little deeper. "I'd think," Slake said, "that you'd want me to fail, given that my failure would mean my soul defaults to you upon my death."

Dyre shrugged. "Either way, I win. Either the clients pay me millions, or I get your soul. Matters little to me, except that the clients have always been good ones, and I'd like to keep them."

As far as Slake was concerned, the clients could go fuck themselves. Whoever they were. With a mental *fuck you*, he escaped the office and hit the nearest Harrowgate, an ancient one that sat behind a stinky-ass fish shop. Before he stepped in, he texted Atrox.

Find out everything you can about a demon named Raze. Medic at Thirst. I want to know about every breath he's taken since the day he was born.

Slake waited, picturing Atrox awkwardly knuckling his phone's keyboard until he finally came back with, *Is this personal or business?*

Just do it.

Personal, then. Gotcha.

Slake cursed under his breath as he typed. *Just do it, jackass.*

:-) I love you too, buddy.

Shaking his head, Slake slipped the phone into his pocket and stepped into the Harrowgate. Instantly, the black walls lit up with symbols for Sheoul, Earth, and Underworld General Hospital. He tapped the Earth symbol, and a map of the entire globe covered the inside of the closet-sized space. He swiped a finger over the glowing continent of Europe, then Germany, then Bavaria, and finally, the Harrowgate nearest his home in the Alps.

The gate opened, and as he stepped out into the dark forest, he sighed with relief. No matter how bad his day was, it always felt good to come back here, to the place no one, not even Atrox, knew about. This was his sanctuary.

But as he trudged through trees to the log cabin sitting high on a bluff, he wondered how much longer it would remain a place of safety.

Because if Dyre claimed his soul, there would be no place on Earth or in Sheoul where he could hide.

Raze should be in bed. He should be sound asleep and resting for his shift at Underworld General in the morning.

Instead, he was sitting at Thirst's bar, letting the cacophony of nightclub life drown out the thoughts in his head.

Seven hours later, Fayle was still in retaliation mode, and this time, she was stretching it to the limit. He needed sex so badly that stabbing pains were starting to feel like tiny daggers in his groin. In another hour, the pain would turn him into a mindless monster that would attack any females near him, and if he still didn't get sex, in another hour he'd be dead. Even now, the females were feeling the effects of his fuck-me pheromones, rubbing up against him and touching themselves, probably without even realizing what they were doing.

It would be so easy to take off with any of these females, but while his cock said yes, his mind couldn't go there until it became too fogged with pain and need. And it wasn't even because of his deal with Fayle. It was because he couldn't stand how it made him feel to have sex with someone he didn't want, simply because biology forced him to. Maybe that made him an idiot, but he wanted control over his mind and his body.

As a particularly severe stab of pain made him suck air, it crossed his mind that maybe holding out until Fayle finally came to him instead of going to her and begging was his way of punishing his body for making him need what he didn't want.

A slinky blonde vampire approached, her hips popping with each step, her fingers trailing up and down between two plump breasts that seemed desperate to escape the tight black corset that bound them.

Raze's cock strained even more against the fly of his jeans, but it was a response based on the need he hated so much, not desire. No, the male vamp sucking on a man near the medic station was far more Raze's type.

So is Slake.

With a growl, Raze reached for his ice water, tempted to dump it on his crotch. Maybe an icy bath would douse the fever starting to spread from his groin.

The female vamp was closer now, her lips parted to reveal two pristine fangs. Suddenly, his field of vision filled with a curvy brunette who made him sigh with relief.

"Hey, my sweet baby," Lexi purred, her thick Irish accent cutting through the other sounds. "Need a save?"

He grinned. Like all of the club employees, she knew he was exclusive with Fayle. But unlike everyone else, she knew the real deal. The lion shifter saw what others didn't, and within a couple months of working at Thirst, she'd started playfully teasing him, pointing out the especially hot guys when they came in. He should have been annoyed, he guessed, but it had been a relief to have someone besides Fayle to talk to.

Fayle didn't feel the same way.

"You're awesome," he said, hugging her to him and taking grim satisfaction in the way the vamp stormed off. He liked Lexi, loved that her bubbly personality concealed a genius IQ she wielded like a weapon, unleashing it now and then to knock arrogant idiots down a few pegs. Watching her tend bar for a bunch of drunk imbeciles who thought she was just a dumb, pretty face was a form of entertainment. "If I were into females . . . and lion shifters . . ."

Laughing, Lexi kissed him on the cheek. "My ass. If one of my brothers walked in here right now, you'd come all over yourself, lion shifter or not."

"If I could do that, I wouldn't need Fayle." He snorted. "Which would be a blessing right now."

Lexi frowned down at him. "What's up her ass this time?"

Not him, that was for sure. Fayle didn't like to be touched. Or kissed. Didn't like her body defiled by sweat and saliva and semen. Only on very rare occasions did she allow him more than a businesslike blowjob. Gods, what he wouldn't give for someone to touch him. To hold him. To kiss him like he was the only person in the world.

The way Slake had done just hours ago.

"Nothing," he muttered.

"I seriously doubt that," Lexi said, gesturing to her fellow bartender. "She's holding out on you over this *nothing*, isn't she?" The bartender handed Lexi a bottle of tequila and a shot glass. She poured a shot as she spoke. "You need to kick that controlling twat to the curb."

"She doesn't do this often, Lex."

Lexi slammed the liquor and poured another. She was on duty, but management didn't care if employees drank, as long as they could keep their shit together. Lexi could down the entire bottle and still win bartending competitions.

"Don't give in to her this time." Lexi dropped her hand to his thigh. "Let me take care of you."

She offered now and then, and he'd been tempted to take her up on it. Lexi could keep sex and love separate, and he knew she'd be more than a robot in bed. But Fayle wouldn't take it well, and he wouldn't put Lexi in her crosshairs.

"I can't," he said roughly, his need growing almost out of control now. Lexi's hand cupping his erection wasn't helping. Neither was the fact that Slake's face kept popping into his mind, as if it was the male massaging his cock instead of Lexi. "Fayle—"

She squeezed him, and he hissed in both pleasure at her touch, and pain at the need to come. Sweat broke out all over his body, and his mind went hazy as instinct began to override his rational thoughts.

"Fayle will get over it," Lexi said.

He shook his head even as he arched into Lexi's hand, and as he did, he got a glimpse of a silky black head of hair whipping around as the female it belonged to stormed toward the rear exit.

Fayle.

Cursing, he peeled Lexi's hand away and stood. "She might get over it, but I'm the one who has to live with her until she does."

"Good luck," Lexi called out as he made his way through the crowd, but he barely heard her over the rush of blood pounding in his ears. His body had control now, and it took every last brain cell he had to maintain forward momentum to the apartment instead of grabbing the closest female and doing her right up against the wall.

The only thing that kept him going now was the thought that by the time he got to their place, he'd be so far gone with lust that *he'd* control the battle of wills that always raged between him and Fayle.

She was ready for him when he burst into the apartment, standing naked in the middle of the room, her clothes draped neatly over the back of the couch. A stranger would see defiance in her wide-legged stance and squared shoulders, but that was all for show.

She smelled of fear.

The incubus inside him would have preferred to smell arousal, but ultimately, he was a demon who had been driven to the very limits of his self-restraint, and the scent of her fear made his blood sing and his cock throb. He wouldn't hurt her, but he wouldn't spare her, either. And he sure as shit wasn't going to let her call the shots. She hated and feared not being in control more than anything, but she'd pushed him too far, and she knew it.

When he took her roughly down to the hard floor and ground his mouth onto hers, she didn't protest.

Not even when he murmured Slake's name against her lips.

CHAPTER FOUR

Slake had dreamed of Raze all night long. Then he'd thought about him all morning as he got his ass ready for the day. Now it was early afternoon, and he was *still* thinking about him.

It pissed him off. He never let his lovers occupy important space in his head, let alone *dreamed* about his lovers . . . or potential lovers. Not since Gunther. Not since Slake had been a different person. *Very* different.

Snarling to himself, he put his vampire ex out of him mind, but he kept Raze front and center as he fondled the smooth length of enchanted rope in his jacket pocket, one of the few objects that could immobilize a demon of Fayle's species. Without it, she could hypnotize him or, if the rumors were accurate, she could shift into a dragon-like beast and swallow him whole.

Not cool.

The Harrowgate he'd entered a moment ago opened, and he stepped out into the bustling emergency department at Underworld General Hospital. He'd never been here before, but like everyone else who didn't live under a rock, he'd heard about it. A hospital run by demons, vampires, and weres that existed under the streets of Manhattan, right under human noses, was sort of a big deal in the underworld community, even if a large percentage thought it was a stupid concept.

Personally, Slake thought that it and its London-based clinic were a good idea, and not even so much for the medical aspect. The hospital and clinic provided jobs and education, not to mention sanctuary, inside their no-violence-allowed walls. Which wasn't to say that UGH's and UGC's staff were a bunch of saints. Apparently, pain meds were optional for patients who were assholes, and the concept of bedside manner was a totally human notion.

Whatever. Slake didn't plan to ever be a patient. Besides, there was only one kind of bedside manner that worked for him, and it damned sure didn't include needles or sutures or antiseptic.

Although . . . he wouldn't mind if "bedside manner" involved a certain male medic.

On the topic of a certain male medic, he did a quick scan of the emergency department. At the reception desk, a vampire was arguing with a chubby, ratlike demon in scrubs, and across the room under rows of caged lights, several patients of varying species waited for their turn to see a doctor. And there, in one of the exam cubicles, his gloved hand resting on a patient's distended abdomen, was Raze. As Slake watched, the glyphs on Raze's arm began to glow, and the female patient cried out before sighing and relaxing.

Raze said something that made her smile weakly. He smiled back and took her hand in his with a tenderness that left Slake in awe. In Slake's world, there was no room for kindness. He showed none and received none. Sometimes, he didn't believe it existed.

But Raze wasn't just doing a job for a paycheck. Clearly, he enjoyed helping others. And just as clearly, Slake thought sourly, Raze had never been in the real world. Anyone who'd seen as much as Slake had lost their sense of empathy.

Raze fiddled with a dial on a machine next to the female's bed and then peeled off his gloves as he exited the cubicle. He waved at someone down the hall, but the moment he saw Slake, he came to an abrupt halt.

"What the fuck are you doing here?" he growled. The grumpy ass.

"A bouncer at Thirst told me you were working here today," Slake said, leaving out the part where he'd had to threaten the bouncer with the loss of vital organs if he didn't cooperate. His threats had probably gotten him banned from Thirst, but whatever. They'd worked. "You have two jobs?"

Raze shrugged, one powerful shoulder rolling under green scrubs embroidered with the Underworld General caduceus symbol, a blade with stylized bat wings circled by two serpents. "I started here a while back, but I work part-time at Thirst. A few of us do both."

A stunning dark-haired demon with arm markings similar to Raze's exited the Harrowgate, the name *Eidolon* stitched onto his white lab coat. Almost simultaneously, another impossibly handsome demon with matching tats came through sliding doors that appeared to lead to an underground parking lot. Although the newest guy wore jeans and a black Star Wars T-shirt, he strode through the place like he owned it, whistling to the tune of Johnny Cash's "Ghost Riders in the Sky," his shoulder-length blond hair brushing against the glyphs on his throat as he walked.

"Damn, there are a lot of you here," Slake said, unable to hide the appreciation in his voice. "Which begs the question . . . what *are* you?"

The blond newcomer slowed, smiled wide enough to reveal fangs, and slapped Raze on the back. "We're Sems."

"What?"

"Seminus demons," he said. "Incubi. We're kind of awesome."

Raze wheeled away to toss his gloves in the trash. "Thanks, Wraith," he said flatly. "You're always so helpful."

Slake looked between Wraith and Raze. "You're sex demons?" The reason for their model-handsome good looks suddenly made a lot of sense, and so did Slake's intense attraction to Raze.

"Yup. Cool, huh?" Wraith gestured to the Seminus demon with the short dark hair. "That's my bro. Raze is related to us somewhere down the arm."

Slake blinked. "Somewhere down the . . . arm?"

"It's really not important," Raze muttered, but Wraith shouldered him out of the way and gestured to the sleeve of tats that began on his right hand and extended all the way to his neck, just like Raze's did.

"It's called a *dermoire*. The glyphs are a paternal history, and we each have our own symbol." Wraith fingered the hourglass symbol just below his jaw at the top of his *dermoire*. "This one is mine. The one below it is my father's. The one below that is my grandfather's. Keeps going. See, this skull glyph belongs to my great-great-great-great-great-grandfather, who happens to be Raze's great-great-great-grandfather."

Slake eyed the two braided tribal rings around Wraith's neck. "Why do you have a glyph around your neck, but Raze doesn't?"

Wraith grinned. "Means I'm mated."

"So there are females of your species?"

"Nope. We reproduce with the females of other species, but our offspring are always purebred Seminus males."

Huh. Slake glanced over at Raze, who seemed extremely engrossed in opening a box of surgical masks. From this angle, Slake couldn't see Raze's personal symbol, but now he wanted to know what it was.

"And you guys are sex demons," he mused. Wasn't *that* curious. He'd never heard of sex demons that went for their same gender, but he knew damned well he hadn't read Raze's signals wrong. He certainly hadn't read the kiss wrong. "So . . . you do males too?"

"Dude." Wraith cringed. "Fuck, no. Females only."

"Really." Slake looked over at Raze again, whose face had gone an interesting shade of red. "No exceptions?"

The Harrowgate flashed open, and Wraith waved at the female wearing a lab coat with the name *Gem* stitched onto the chest pocket in big loopy, multicolored swirls, her blue-streaked black hair pulled up in twin pigtails. "Other males can participate, but—"

"Slake, can I talk to you?" Raze ground out from between clenched teeth. "Outside?"

"'S'okay," Wraith said. "I gotta catch Eidolon before he gets busy helping people and crap. Later."

The moment Wraith sauntered off, Raze grabbed Slake, and the next thing he knew, he was being dragged into the parking lot. The manhandling was something he'd normally beat the shit out of someone for, but as Raze threw him up against a concrete pillar and got in his face, all he wanted to do was kiss the guy. Continue what they'd started in the alley behind Thirst.

"No more questions," Raze growled, the low, breathy sound rumbling through all of Slake's erogenous zones.

Then realization dawned. "Your friends don't know, do they? They have no idea you're into males."

Gold flecks, like sunlight glinting off a lake of emerald, glinted in Raze's eyes. "What the fuck did I just say?"

In a quick motion, Slake gripped Raze's shoulders and spun him around so it was Raze's spine biting into the post. Before the incubus could recover, Slake covered his mouth with his own. Raze froze, his body taut, his teeth clenched behind lips as cold and unyielding as the pillar. Slake kept up the pressure for a few seconds, making it clear that he didn't give up easily.

Point made, he put his mouth to Raze's ear and whispered, "Was that why you broke it off last night? Right when things were getting good?" Never mind that Slake had been about to do the same. "Because you don't want anyone to know you're into guys?"

"It's a little more complicated than that." Raze tried to shove Slake away, but he held his ground, pulling back only enough to look the guy in the eye. "Actually, a lot more complicated."

Slake understood that, since he wasn't exactly a typical, shining example of his own species. "Tell me."

Raze snorted. "You gonna share *your* trauma first? I didn't think so. So step off, asshole."

Gods, this guy was hot when he was pissed. Slake had never been one for angry sex, but something about Raze made him want to tear off both of their clothes and make use of the hood on that new BMW behind them.

He was about to say as much when the hospital's sliding doors opened and two paramedics rushed out, heading for one of two black ambulances parked nearby. One, a blond guy with eerie silver eyes, shouted at Raze.

"It's Thirst," he yelled. "Some kind of explosion."

Slake's heart skidded to a panicked stop in his chest. If Fayle had been injured or killed, he was in a shit-ton of trouble. The muffled trill of a phone ringing jumpstarted his heart again, and then Raze had his cell to his ear.

"Yeah, shit, I'll be right there." He pocketed the phone and tore away from Slake. "I gotta go."

"I'm going with you."

"Whatever," Raze said. "But get in my way and I'll send you back here—in the back of that ambulance."

Slake almost laughed. Almost. Because if Fayle was dead, being in the back of an ambulance would be far preferable to whatever punishment Dyre could come up with.

Raze had always prided himself on his ability to remain calm during a crisis. To put fear on the back burner when things were crazy. But as he leaped out of the Harrowgate next to Thirst with Slake on his heels, terror pumped through him. Images of his parents, torn apart by demons, flashed in his head, and he knew he'd see the same kind of trauma in the bombing victims. Victims who were his friends. Marsden, Lexi, Vladlena . . . Fayle.

Oh gods, no.

The acrid stench of death made him gag as he stepped over chunks of jagged debris, his palm sweating all over the handle of the medic bag he'd grabbed from UGH.

Chaos ruled the scene, chaos and charred bricks and twisted, mangled metal. Sirens and screams rent the air, which was thick with black, ashy smoke that stung his eyes and nostrils. New York City emergency responders scrambled to treat the humans who had been caught in the blast that had ripped apart both Thirst and the strictly human club that served as its front.

Nate, wasn't stupid, though, and he'd already deployed the mystics he kept on staff to alter human memories when needed. The last thing anyone wanted was a paramedic or cop coming across injured demons or discovering a vampire club in their own human backyard.

"Damn." Slake's soft voice came from right next to Raze, but somehow it seemed distant, as if there was no place for anything here but screams.

"Come on," he barked, sprinting toward Thirst's blast-warped side door.

A few feet away, one of the mystics, Jen, was doing her, *These aren't the droids you're looking for* thing to a firefighter who had been heading toward the same door, now visible to humans thanks to a failure in the concealment spell that kept the place hidden from human eyes.

Inside was . . . shit. Smoke clogged the air and soot covered the destroyed furniture, walls, and every piece of broken glass that littered the floor next to the bodies of the dead and injured.

Pained moans and cries for help spurred Raze into action. Heart pounding, he frantically searched the victims, hoping his friends weren't among them. Hoping Fayle wasn't among them. She generally avoided the club, preferring to collect the sexual energy she needed to survive from quieter sources. But every once in a while, if she needed a quick fix, the club offered sexual vibes in spades.

As he kneeled next to a goat-demon and pressed his palm against a spurting wound in the male's furry leg, he heard a female voice call out his name, and he gave a mental sigh of relief.

"Raze." Fayle stood near the destroyed medic station, her face pale, but she was otherwise unharmed. "I was in the apartment when I heard the blast. What can I do?"

She was useless around blood, fainting at the sight of anything more than a paper cut, but it was cool of her to offer. "Go back to the apartment and wait for me. I'll be there as soon as I can."

"What about me?" Slake called out from where he was crouched over one of the vampire waitresses, Ava, as she rested against a wall, her mangled arm held protectively against her chest. "What do you need me to do?"

Raze eyed Slake, the bulge of weapons beneath his jacket, and wondered what the guy did for a living. Somehow, Raze suspected Slake was more likely to be the person who caused injuries than fixed them.

"Get Ava to Underworld General Clinic. All the walking wounded need to go there. We'll let the hospital handle the critical patients." He increased pressure on his patient's wound while he used his other hand to gesture to his medic bag. "And grab some triage tags and black flag any DRT you come across."

"DRT?"

Right. Slake wouldn't understand the medical slang. "Dead Right There. Deceased," he clarified. "Tag 'em as you come across them. It'll save medical personnel time." And it would give Slake something useful to do while he searched for walking wounded to escort to the clinic.

Slake leaped into action as Raze turned back to his patient. "Hey, buddy," he said in his calmest medic voice. "What's your name?"

"B-Blead."

"Like bleed," Raze said, keeping his tone light. The guy was going to be okay, but without Raze, he'd bleed out. "What you're doing right now."

"Funny . . . guy," Blead gasped, his goatlike snout wrinkling as a wave of pain wracked him.

Quickly, Raze engaged his healing power to reduce the guy's bleeding. Energy surged through his arm, running along his *dermoire* in a pulsing tingle instead of a steady buzz. Son of a bitch, he was running low on juice after six busy hours at the hospital.

Instead of doing a full heal, he did a partial, enough to keep the guy alive until one of the uninjured staff members could escort Blead to one of Underworld General's facilities.

For the rest of the afternoon, he was forced to use his gift sparingly, moving from patient to patient to triage and heal the most severe and life-threatening injuries so that the other arriving UG medical staff could treat and transport to the hospital.

He hated triage. Always had. Every instinct in him screamed for him to heal his patients, to stay with them until he was confident they were out of danger. But mass casualty situations didn't allow for that, and he lost track of the number of times he had to pause for a few seconds to rein in his frustration.

He also lost track of time as he worked. Every once in a while he'd catch sight of Slake as he helped rescuers haul heavy debris off victims or offered comfort to the injured. Once, Slake even saved a life by tying a tourniquet around a human's leg that had been blown off at the knee. Where Slake had found the rope he'd used, Raze had no idea, but it was good thinking.

A couple of times, Raze found himself admiring the way Slake handled the situation with confidence and authority, while still obeying orders from rescue personnel. Impressive, how he was able to keep his ego in check. Raze had figured Slake to be the kind of muscle-bound, arrogant warrior who would balk at taking instruction. So he was hot *and* smart.

Knock it off. You're only setting yourself up for disaster.

Not to mention that he kept drooling over another male in the *middle* of a disaster. So. Damned. Inappropriate.

Cursing himself, Raze wiped his brow on his sleeve and got back to it. The frantic pace of the emergency finally wound down as evening settled in, but as he helped another of Wraith and Eidolon's brothers, a paramedic named Shade, wheel a patient out to the waiting ambulance, he heard Slake shout for help.

He ran back inside, but he didn't see Slake anywhere among the scorched and mangled debris. "Where are you?"

"Over here!"

Raze threaded his way to the far corner of the building and found Slake kneeling behind an overturned table, his voice low and soothing as he spoke to someone Raze couldn't see. When he got closer, Raze's heart stuttered at the sight of a female form lying on the floor, her lower half crushed beneath a massive section of wall. Slake was holding a frail hand in one palm as he tenderly brushed long brunette hair out of the female's blood-streaked face.

Lexi.

"It'll be okay," Slake murmured, his tone hesitant and awkward, as if he wasn't used to promising hope. "I won't leave you. I swear."

Lexi's golden-brown eyes were glazed with pain and shock, but she locked onto Slake's gaze with the fierceness that only a lion shifter could manage. "Thank you," she rasped. "Thank . . . you."

"No." Raze's voice sounded as destroyed as the club as he sank heavily to his knees. "*No!*"

He gripped Lexi's biceps and channeled what was left of his power into her, but a heartbeat later it became clear that she was beyond his capacity to help, even if his ability had been fully charged. He felt her drift away, her pulse becoming weaker as his pounded harder, until it stopped completely and her beautiful eyes clouded over.

"Ah damn," he whispered.

"I'm sorry," Slake said softly. "I didn't know what to do—"

"You did everything you could." Raze shuddered, but long after it should have stopped, his body continued to tremble. He couldn't let go of Lexi, not until Slake pried his fingers from her limp arm.

"Come on, Raze." Slake signaled to a team of rescue personnel as he pulled Raze to his feet. "Let them do what they need to do."

Raze nodded numbly, grateful for the way Slake had taken over and given him a chance to step back. He was also grateful for the way Slake stood protectively close, his hand a comforting, steady presence on Raze's shoulder.

"I liked her," Raze said, his voice as thick as the smoke that lingered in the air. "I liked her a lot." He looked at the trashed club, at the pools of blood that mingled with the soot and ash, and without an adrenaline rush and victims to treat, the reality of the situation finally sank in. "So much death and destruction. Why?"

Slake shook his head. "Looks like Thirst took the bulk of the blast. At first, I thought the human club was the target, but if you look over there—" he pointed to the restrooms "—you can see where the blast originated. It was also focused, so it blew toward the front of the club. Someone wanted to take out the club without taking out the entire building. In fact . . ."

Slake's voice became a muted buzz, until all Raze heard was, *blah, blah, maybe humans did it, blah, blah, inspect the materials used, blah, blah, blahblahblahblahblah . . .*

"Blah."

Raze felt himself being shaken.

"*Blah*!"

More shaking.

"*Raze*!"

He blinked. Focused. Slake was standing in front of him, expression tight with concern, his hands on Raze's shoulders.

"Raze, man, you okay?"

"Yeah." No. Someone had intentionally maimed and killed dozens of people. How could he be okay with that? Making matters worse, as his adrenaline waned, his body was going through alternating hot and cold flashes, and his gut was starting to ache as the first symptoms of sexual withdrawal began. He glanced down at his watch. It was nearly 7 p.m., a little over twelve hours since Fayle had given him a release that had been so cold and clinical they might as well have been at UGH's fertility clinic instead of their own apartment. He had no idea how long she was going to punish him for taking all of the control away from her last night, but he did know he'd need her again soon. Very soon.

But right now, as he looked into Slake's eyes, he needed something else. He wasn't even sure what. All he knew was that Slake was the key.

"Come with me." Raze started walking, wondering if Slake would follow.

It wasn't until he reached the door that led to his upstairs apartment that he heard the heavy strike of Slake's boots behind him.

CHAPTER FIVE

Slake followed Raze to an apartment across the way from Thirst, his steps leaden with exhaustion. At over a century old, Slake had seen a lot of violence—had been the *cause* of a lot of violence—but he'd never let himself get sucked into an emotional involvement.

Sure, over the years he'd lost a lot of friends and lovers, but he'd learned the hard way to never get too attached, and even more importantly, to never be affected by anyone else's attachments. To never feel empathy. Or even sympathy. Life was hard, and it only got harder when you had more to care about than just yourself. Inevitably, those you cared about had a nasty habit of kicking you in the nuts when they couldn't accept who you were.

But seeing Raze so affected by his failure to save everyone, especially a friend, had rattled something loose inside him. The guy had been stoic and professional from the moment they'd arrived on scene, but in the last five minutes, the hard shell surrounding Raze had cracked—as much a victim of the bombing as Thirst had been—and Slake found himself wanting to fix it.

Weird, considering that Slake had been born to a species of demon that was all about destruction and suffering. Of course, the fact that Slake had never fit in was exactly why he'd left them behind.

Still, his people might be barbaric and primitive, but there was something to be said for not giving a shit about anyone else's pain. Even now, when Slake should have been doing what he always did and mentally preparing himself for the worst thing that could possibly happen once he stepped inside Raze's apartment, he was wondering what he could do to erase the shadows that haunted Raze's gorgeous green eyes.

Raze led Slake inside a small but neat apartment that appeared to be part of a converted factory floor. Thick metal pillars made for interesting obstacles, but at least they'd been painted in bright primary colors that matched the Ikea furniture and modern art on the walls. Soft jazz music drifted from what Slake assumed was a bedroom, but Raze took a sharp left and made a beeline for the kitchen. Slake started after him, but movement in the bedroom doorway caught his attention.

Halting, he swung his head around. A female was watching him, her black hair falling over her face so he could only see one eye, but that one eye was narrowed, full of suspicion.

Fayle. No question about it. He'd seen enough pictures—and one extremely detailed drawing provided by the law firm's client—to recognize her.

He watched her until she pivoted around and disappeared back into the bedroom. Complete with a door slam.

For a split second he wondered what would happen if he hadn't used the bindings intended for her to stop an injured dude's bleeding, and instead barged into her room, grabbed her, and packaged her for delivery to Dire & Dyre. How much of a battle would Raze put up? Would he be forced to kill the guy?

Slake had always been careful to avoid collateral damage, but his soul was on the line, and he'd do what he had to do. But damn it, something about Raze made him want to figure out another way. Or, at least, to stall a little. Fayle would still be here tomorrow.

Probably.

Cursing himself for a fool, he entered the kitchen . . . and stopped dead. Raze stood at the sink, his scrub top wadded on the floor, leaving him tantalizingly nude from the waist up. His muscles rolled and flexed under the supple skin of his back as he washed the blood and soot from his hands and arms.

Damn. Slake swallowed dryly, unable to tear his gaze away. And when Raze finally grabbed a hand towel and wiped himself down, all Slake could think about was how lucky that piece of cloth was. And how his tongue could do a much better job.

Raze tossed the towel to the floor next to his soot-and-blood-streaked top and yanked open the fridge door. "Beer?"

Somehow, Slake managed a casual shrug and a scratchy, "Sure."

Raze tossed him a bottle of some fancy microbrew, and then he twisted the cap off his own and drained half the contents.

"Thought you didn't drink."

Closing his eyes, Raze kicked his head back against the blue-tiled wall. The muscles in his throat rippled as he swallowed, and Slake suddenly imagined himself kissing his way down that long, arched neck. Imagined tracing the symbol under his jaw with his tongue. Imagined the sounds Raze would make while he was doing it. Gods, the very thought made heat rush to his groin and his heart race startlingly fast.

Slake wanted Raze in a way he hadn't wanted anyone in a long, long time.

"I can't get drunk, but drinking still makes me want what I can't have." Rake's lids lifted, and Slake's muscles went rubber at the dark hunger that gleamed in the depths of his eyes. "Right now, what I want is standing in front of me, and I'm pretty sure I can have it." His voice went low. Smoky. Sexy as fuck. "Am I right?"

Holy shit. A tight fist of heat clenched in his chest and spread in a slow wave as his body reacted to the blatant promise of raw sex. He eyed Raze and those magnificent shoulders and thick arms that were built to hold a partner steady for an onslaught of bliss. Lower, his broad chest tapered down to rippling, hard abs and a narrow waist that disappeared into pants that did nothing to hide an impressive erection.

Gods, to have all that solid strength beneath him, absorbing his thrusts . . .

"You're right," Slake said roughly, even as what Wraith had said earlier echoed in his head. "But Wraith said your kind only does females, and I just saw one in your living room."

Raze took a step closer, the glittery flecks in his eyes melting together like liquid gold. "I'll die without sex. Sex with females. She keeps me alive, and I do the same for her."

"But you can still have sex with males, right?" *Please say yes. Please say yes.*

"As long as a female is present, yes." He took another step closer, his shoulders rolling, and Slake's cock jerked.

"Present? Like, nearby?"

The tent in Raze's scrubs grew even more pronounced, and Slake's mouth watered. "Present, as in we have to ejaculate into one."

"So . . . you're bisexual?"

"Does it matter?" Raze said softly, the heat in his voice an almost tangible warmth that settled on Slake's skin like a fever.

Suddenly, Slake didn't care if the guy was into males, females, or two-headed asexual purple snake demons. All that mattered was closing the distance between them.

In an instant, Slake was no longer standing across the room from Raze. He was chest to chest, mouth to mouth, hard cock to hard cock.

Raze met him with equal enthusiasm, thrusting his tongue against Slake's as he wrapped an arm around his waist and wheeled them both into the adjacent room. Which, thank fuck, turned out to be a bedroom.

Slake didn't question Raze's motives in bringing him here after being so adamant about not wanting him. He took control the way he always did, pushing Raze onto the bed. Raze complied, lying back to allow Slake to pull off his scrub pants and boxer briefs. Slake practically drooled at the sight of Raze's erection jutting up from between his legs, the dusky column of flesh curved against his hard belly.

Man, Raze was a work of art, a study of male perfection right down to the raw, wild intensity in his gold-flecked gaze.

Slake was not going to draw this out. He wanted it way too much.

Making quick work of his clothes, he lunged onto the bed. Raze arched his hips as Slake opened his mouth over the head of his cock and swirled his tongue around the crown.

"Yes," Raze whispered. "Touch me."

Like Slake needed to be told. Gripping Raze's hips, he licked his way down his thick shaft until he reached the heavy sac at the base. Raze sucked in a harsh breath as Slake pressed the tip of his tongue against the seam dividing the two firm testicles.

As Slake sucked and licked Raze's balls, he wrapped one hand around Raze's cock and squeezed. Raze groaned, and Slake's dick pulsed as if reminding him that it needed attention.

He let go of Raze and gripped his own erection as he worked his way back up, tracing the dark veins that read like a roadmap of ecstasy on Raze's shaft. A silky drop of pre-cum dripped from the tip, and Slake eagerly captured it with his mouth, and this time it was his turn to groan. The salty, slightly spicy taste coated his tongue, and heat spread through his insides as he swallowed.

Damn, it was almost like downing a few shots of whiskey, the way every inch of his body became sensitized. At this point, Raze could probably caress Slake's *elbow* and give him an orgasm.

Sex demons were awesome.

Nearly lost to lust, he looked up, meeting Raze's hot gaze. Such a fucking turn-on to see that same want, that *need*, spreading through his eyes in splashes of molten gold. "Your eyes," he rasped. "I love how they change color."

"The gold comes out when I'm turned on." Raze arched his hips, rubbing his erection on Slake's chin and lips. "Or when I'm angry."

Slake swirled his tongue around the crown of Raze's cock, loving how Raze hissed in pleasure. "I like it. I want to see more."

Raze slung an arm to the side to fumble with the bedside drawer, where he drew out a bottle of lube. Slake's cock throbbed in agonizing response.

"What about the female?" Slake breathed, pretending he didn't know who she was. And at this point, he didn't care. He couldn't, or an emotion he wasn't used to might rear its ugly head.

Guilt.

Raze gripped Slake's hair and roughly tugged him up his body. "Fayle will join us when I need her."

Slake reminded himself to ask later how she'd know. Right now, all he wanted was to bury himself balls-deep inside Raze.

With an impatient snarl, Slake jammed his arm beneath Raze's shoulders to flip him, but Raze stopped him with an iron grip on his biceps. Raze lifted his mouth to Slake's ear and took his lobe between his teeth hard enough to make Slake hiss.

Raze licked the spot, soothing it, and then in a voice dripping with lust, he said, "You smell like sex. Power. It's making me so hard it hurts. If I could, I'd have you bent over that chair behind you, and I'd drill you so hard you'd feel me for days."

Ah . . . *yes*. Slake spread his thighs as Raze's hand delved between them, finding his shaft, then going lower, to his balls, and when his fingertips found the sensitive patch just behind them, Slake tilted his hips to give Raze access to anything he wanted.

Slake had always preferred to do the drilling, as Raze had put it, but something about Raze made him want to experience being taken by a powerful, intense male who was literally made for sex.

Before Raze, he'd only felt that way about one other person, and even then, Slake's sexual position on the bottom had been a requirement of their relationship, the only way Gunther would do it.

And damn it, why did that bastard have to intrude on what was happening right here, right now, with a male Gunther couldn't even begin to compare to?

Mentally staking his vampire ex-lover, Slake shoved Raze roughly back into the mattress. "You'll be the one feeling me, incubus," he growled as he flipped Raze and covered him, pushing his erection between his muscular thighs.

Ah damn, he was not going to last long even like this. Somehow Raze knew, pushing himself up on his hands and knees so Slake's cock was poised at his entrance.

Raze tossed the bottle of lube into the air. Slake caught it one-handed, and in a matter of seconds, he was pushing slowly past the tight ring of muscle. His sex throbbed as he eased inside Raze's hot hole, and finally, gods finally, he was seated to the hilt.

Unable to wait another second, he withdrew… and then slammed his hips forward. Raze moaned, the sound swallowed by Slake's own breathy groan.

Ecstasy rolled through him. Holy hell, this was unbelievable. Every inch of Raze's body was made for this, which wasn't a surprise, given that he was a sex demon, but still, the way his ass clenched around Slake's cock, rippling from the base to the head… fuck.

He barely heard the sound of soft footsteps, realizing at the last second that Fayle had entered the room. He froze, embarrassed and angry at himself for letting his lust get in the way of maintaining a measure of awareness for everything going on around him. Then Raze pushed against him, and hey, it wasn't as if Fayle was brandishing an ax and wearing armor. Even if she had, his weapons were in reach. They were always within reach.

But no, she was empty-handed, dressed the way she had been earlier, in black yoga pants and a yellow fitted T-shirt that showcased full breasts and a hard belly, and she didn't look happy to be here. In fact, when she glanced at Slake, she curled her lip in a silent snarl, letting him know that if he had any intention of touching her, he'd best forget it.

Message received, but unnecessary. Slake had never been into females—to the murderous disappointment of his family.

Beneath him, Raze shifted, straightening up so his back plastered against Slake's chest. Slake hissed at the new sensation from the upright position. Raze ground his ass against him, and the release boiling in his balls went critical. Clenching his teeth, he concentrated on holding it back as Fayle climbed onto the mattress, facing Raze on her hands and knees, and took his hard length in her mouth.

Jealousy screamed through Slake. He wanted to be the one to make Raze come. To make the guy shout to whatever deity he worshipped.

"Fuck me," Raze groaned. "Do it. Hard."

Oh hell yeah. Slake gripped Raze's hip in one hand and slipped the other around to his sternum to brace him as he drew back his own hips and slammed them forward, nearly lifting Raze off the bed with the force of his thrust.

Raze groaned again, and Slake did it harder. Harder, until the only sound in the room was flesh slapping against flesh and panting breaths.

Slake's balls went tight, the orgasm rolling through his cock until he exploded in a mind-blowing storm of sensation. It went on and on, and then, just as it died down, Raze shouted, his ass clenching, and Slake joined in for another release that shattered him more thoroughly than the first one. A third followed on its heels, draining him of everything, including energy and thoughts.

They collapsed onto the mattress, Slake shifting to the side so he wouldn't crush Raze. It was only then that he realized Fayle had slipped away.

Good riddance. It was going to be a pleasure to deliver her to Dire & Dyre.

CHAPTER SIX

Raze didn't know how long he lay in bed, unable to move, as helpless as a baby Sem. Slake could kill him right now, and all Raze could do about it would be to first thank him for the best orgasm of his life.

He'd been with males before, a couple of times, but it had always been awkward. Either they hadn't liked having a female involved, or if they did, they were disappointed that Fayle wouldn't touch anyone but Raze.

Slake didn't seem to give a shit either way.

They were still connected, an intimacy Raze had never shared with anyone. Not even Fayle. When they had sex, it was all about keeping Raze alive and giving her the kind of sexual rush her species needed to survive—a rush she didn't even need to be in the same room to get. Her species was all about proximity to sex, about soaking up energy that radiated from the act of pleasure. Hell, Fayle generally *avoided* sex. Said it was messy. Annoying.

He smiled at the way his damp skin stuck to Slake's. Messy, absolutely. Annoying? Hell no.

Slake slung his arm over Raze's waist and brushed his knuckles back and forth along Raze's rib cage. "That was . . ."

"Yeah," Raze croaked. "It was. I can't move. How are you moving?"

He felt Slake's lips curve into a smile against his shoulder blade. "How is it that I was able to have multiple orgasms with you?"

Raze frowned, uncertain of the answer. "I'm not sure about males, but females always do. Our semen causes them to come over and over, for as long as half an hour."

"Ah, well, I was sort of on the wrong side of you for that."

Interesting. None of his other male partners had experienced that. He wondered if anyone had ever tested the effects of Seminus semen on males of various species. If anyone had, it was Eidolon. Not that he knew how to approach that subject.

Hey, Doc, I had sex with a dude, and he had multiple orgasms, and now I'm curious about our effects on males.

Yeah . . . no.

"So . . . is Fayle in her room right now having some happy time?"

Raze snorted. "Ingesting our semen has a different effect. Makes females horny." Maybe it was his imagination, but he could have sworn Slake stiffened a little. "But Fayle is a succubus that feeds off sexual energy. For her, semen is like a super-concentrated shot of fuel."

Slake licked his throat, a slow swipe along his jugular, and Raze shivered with pleasure. "How often do you need her?"

"Depends." He silently encouraged Slake to lick him again, but he settled for the gentle stroke of his palm along his arm. Gods, how long had it been since someone had touched him like that? "Most Seminus demons need sex several times a day."

Slake's hand froze. "Holy shit. How do you guys get anything done?"

Raze chuckled, but the sound of a siren outside reminded him of the tragedy that had led to this, and he sobered. He wasn't sure why losing his friend, co-workers, and the club he'd grown to feel as comfortable in as his own apartment had made him want to lose himself in Slake, but it wasn't something he was ready to explore.

"The frequency reduces as we get older or after we take a mate. Frequency is also affected by our mother's species." He bit back a contented sigh as Slake resumed the stroking. "I don't know what species my mother was, but she must have been a species with a slow metabolism or that doesn't breed often, because I can go twelve to sixteen hours without sex, but things start getting uncomfortable after about thirteen or fourteen."

"Do Seminus demons take on many traits of your mother's species?" Slake's hand stilled again for a heartbeat before resuming the slow, light strokes. "Or are you guys all alike? Is there such a thing as a half-breed?"

Raze closed his eyes and reveled in being touched. In being alive.

Unlike Lexi.

"No," he said softly. "As long as the mother is a demon, all Seminus demons are purebred. And male." Well, there was an exception to the "males only" rule, but only one. And that *one*, Sin, was sister to the Seminus brothers who'd founded Underworld General. "We take on some minor traits of our mothers, but for the most part, all Sems are representative of our species. If we survive to our hundredth birthday, we become fertile. If we haven't taken a mate by then, we all turn into monsters who can shapeshift to resemble almost any similarly sized species. Then we run around tricking and impregnating every female we see. And like I said, unless the mother is human, the infants are always purebred Sems. It's part of why we're so rare. The females give birth and realize they were tricked and that the baby isn't their species, and they usually abandon or kill the infant."

"Ouch," Slake murmured, his lips brushing Raze's shoulder. "But for being so rare, your hospital is crawling with you guys."

"That's because Eidolon actively searches us out, and he's made UG a safe haven for Sems. Our innate healing abilities make us natural medics and doctors. Trust me, most demons can live five hundred years and never run into one of us."

"So you guys are purebred, but you said the mother's species plays some sort of role in who you are? Like what?"

He inhaled the musky scent of sex and sweat, letting himself enjoy the moment as he shared his species's particulars with Slake. He wasn't used to people being curious about him, and he liked it. "There's a paramedic at Underworld General, Shade . . . his mother was an Umber demon, so he can turn into shadow in the presence of shadow. Wraith's mother was a vampire, so he needs to drink blood. That kind of thing."

Slake's fingers trailed along Raze's hip, and he had to bite back a moan of pleasure that wasn't even sexual. It was . . . appreciative. "Vamps can't breed."

"Long story." Long and weird and Raze didn't want to talk about Wraith right now. He didn't want any males in this bed besides the one he already had spooning him.

"So how is it that you don't know what species your mother was?"

He smiled, remembering his strange, but loving childhood. "I was raised by humans."

"Humans?" Slake sounded like he'd bitten into a lemon. "How did that happen?"

Raze shrugged. "My birth mother abandoned me in a sewer. Left me to be eaten by whoever came along. A couple of Aegis demon hunters found me."

"The *Aegis* found you?" Slake's voice now sounded a little strangled. "And they didn't kill you? That's what those bastards *do*."

The Aegis, an ancient league of human demon slayers, had been the enemy of every underworld being for centuries. But, like all organizations, it had gone through changes over the years, which included reform and even a recent upheaval when members who were sympathetic to non-evil demons rebelled against the old ways. Eidolon had even mated one of their members. So had Gem.

Unfortunately, the recent near-apocalypse had revealed the existence of demons, and The Aegis's numbers were swelling as humans flocked to the righteous cause of destroying what they didn't understand. Not that there weren't a lot of evil demons out there. But there were decent demons too, and a wide range of demons who walked a neutral line.

"At the time The Aegis rescued me, they didn't know I was a demon," Raze said.

"The fact that a newborn had tats on his arm wasn't a clue?"

"I think they knew something was up, but lucky for me, they weren't the typical kill-first-and-ask-questions-later kind of Aegis scumbags. When they couldn't figure out what I was, one of them decided to keep me. She married a doctor when I was three, left The Aegis, and they raised me as their own."

Raze smiled at the memory. Carrie Ann and Ryan Bertrand had given him a good life—a normal life in a human household, which had gone a long way toward giving Raze a more human outlook on the world than many of his demon brethren.

Slake used a fingertip to trace the swirly skull glyph on Raze's wrist, and he shivered at the sensation of having such a sensitive area touched. Caressed. "How did they explain the artwork?"

"My mom made up a story about adopting me from out of an abusive situation. Hell, until I reacted badly to a vaccine and my dad ran some blood tests, even he believed that I'd been born to addicts who got me tattooed as an infant."

"Did you believe it?"

He captured Slake's fingers with his, letting himself play with them as he spoke. The intimacy in such a small thing was stunning, warming him even more than Slake's body plastered against his back.

"I didn't have any reason not to," he said. "Plus, it was kind of cool. All the other kids thought I was a total badass."

Slake shifted, losing the connection between them, and Raze experienced the strangest twinge of disappointment.

"When did the ball drop?" The mattress bounced as Slake rolled out of it. "Because you know it did."

"Oh yeah. It dropped." Raze salivated at the sight of Slake's muscular ass flexing as he disappeared into the bathroom. "Seminus demons don't have any special powers or abilities until they go through the first of two maturation cycles. So everything was cool until I turned twenty and the first one hit."

Fuck, that had been crazy. He'd graduated from high school at sixteen, so he'd been in his fourth year of college, preparing for a career in medicine like his father, when he'd gotten sick. Real sick.

"My vision started blurring, and I was getting these splitting headaches. They got so bad that I couldn't go to any of my college classes, so I went home. My dad ran a free clinic in Los Angeles, so I helped out until the sickness became so debilitating that I couldn't even walk. My mom used her Aegis background to research my symptoms, and she figured out that I was a sex demon of some sort."

Slake spoke over the rush of water in the sink. "She knew you needed sex."

He snorted. "Talk about awkward, huh?" He tucked his arm behind his head and gazed up at the ceiling, not giving a shit that he was naked and sprawled out on the bed. "She was cool, though. She and some of her former Aegis buddies crashed a demon brothel and got a female for me. That female was Fayle."

"And she's been with you ever since?"

"Yup."

The water shut off. "What happens if you go too long?"

"Fever. Agony. Death."

"Well, that's not cool," Slake called out. "So where are your parents now?"

A heavy ache centered in Raze's chest, and it took a moment before he could choke out one simple, yet devastating word. "Dead."

Slake appeared in the doorway, his magnificent body still glistening with sweat. "I'm sorry," he said. "What happened?"

Raze studied the ceiling again. It was pretty unremarkable as far as ceilings went. "The apocalypse shit that went down a couple of years ago."

"Aw, fuck." Slake stepped out of the bathroom, and Raze figured he was heading for his clothes, so he was surprised as hell when Slake stretched out next to him on the bed again. They weren't touching, but this was still the most private, most intimate moment he'd ever shared with anyone, including Fayle.

The knowledge left him off-balance, would probably have freaked him out if they hadn't been chin-deep in conversation about the worst period in Raze's life. He wasn't used to sharing, not because he was an overly private person, but because, besides Lexi, he'd really not had anyone to talk to. His life was work and sex. Sex and work.

Keeping busy kept him from wishing for things he couldn't have. Like a male partner.

Like Slake.

"They were killed during the upheaval. I tried to save them . . ." Raze trailed off, the memory of finding their remains, scattered all over their house, still too fresh to open that wound. He looked over at Slake, who was lying on his side, propped up by one elbow. "What about you? Where's your family?"

Slake's dark eyes iced over. "As far as I know, they're alive and kicking in their special little isolated compound in Sheoul."

"I'm guessing there's a long story and some bad blood there?"

"You could say that."

Yawning, Raze closed his eyes, content to bask in the afterglow of the sex and the surprisingly . . . pleasant conversation. "What do you do for a living, anyway?"

"I work for a law firm."

Raze cracked his lids just enough to eyeball his bedmate. "You're a lawyer?"

Slake barked out a laugh. "Hell no. My species, Duosos, are weapons specialists. We make and control weapons no one else can, like my handy little *sinispheres*. I work for Dire & Dyre, using my skills however they need me to. Mainly because, like an idiot, I signed a contract decades ago that ties me to them until the end of next week."

"What happens at the end of next week?"

"I'm a free agent." There was a note of hesitation in his voice, but Raze didn't want to pry. Not into that, anyway. He was too curious about something else.

"So . . . when you say you're a free agent . . ." He trailed off, gave himself a heartbeat to get his head in the right place, the way he always did before making the first cut of a delicate operation. "Does that apply to relationships?"

Slake sucked in a harsh breath, and Raze immediately regretted the question. He wasn't sure why he'd even asked. It wasn't as if he was available, not when Fayle made being with anyone difficult.

"I'm not with anyone," Slake said slowly, "if that's what you mean." He turned his head to stare at Raze. "What about you? I mean, I know you've got this thing with Fayle, but have you ever tried being with a male without her?"

Raze sighed. "Right after I went through the maturation phase I told you about, I tried to come with a guy. It didn't work."

He'd hoped, had prayed to a hundred different deities he didn't even believe in, but right when his climax had been imminent, so hot it burned, pleasure had abruptly shifted to bone-searing agony. Fayle had been there to help, and she'd never let him forget it.

"But if you found the right guy, could you, I don't know, do a threesome kind of thing? Have you ever tried?"

Raze nearly laughed. Once, he'd been hopeful that somehow he and Fayle could work something out. That somewhere out there was a guy who could accept his arrangement with Fayle, and that she could accept Raze's desire for someone else.

He'd been such a fool.

"We've done the threesome thing a handful of times, but it was all casual. I've never found a male worth trying to break through her jealousy for a real relationship." He glanced at Slake, wondering if maybe, just maybe, he could be the first. Yeah, it was way too soon to start thinking about the future, but damn it, he'd never experienced this kind of intimacy with anyone, and while it wasn't like him to share all of this shit, it felt . . . right.

Slake scowled. "How can she be jealous if she doesn't want you for more than sex?"

"She says her species focuses on ownership." He was surprised by the bitterness in his voice, but then, he was getting tired of playing her games. "They're possessive of everything they consider theirs. They won't even give a friend a meal if they're starving. Sharing some things is punishable by death."

"Why the hell do you put up with it? Why don't you tell her to take a hike?"

"I've tried to leave her," Raze admitted. "I made it a month before I nearly died." His body tightened as if it too remembered being in extraordinary pain and misery. "Most of my kind are natural charmers. They love females and can talk one out of their panties in about ten seconds. But I'm not like that. I spent every waking second trying to figure out how I was going to get sex when I needed it, and I hated fucking strange females. I hated myself, and the stress was killing me. I'd go too long between releases, and then I'd get violent and sick . . . until I took it too far one night and collapsed in a filthy alley behind a hound-hump." He shuddered at the memory of waking up outside the werewolf brothel, his body burning with fever, his eyes bleeding, and Fayle sucking his cock. Somehow, she'd found him and saved his life once again. "My life with Fayle isn't ideal, but it's better than the alternative."

"I guess I can see that." Slake's expression was troubled. "But she's keeping you from being happy."

"Happy?" Raze snorted. "I gave up wishing for that a long time ago. I take what I can get."

Something flickered in Slake's dark eyes. Sadness, maybe? "That doesn't sound like any way to live."

Raze looked up at the ceiling again. "I've accepted my lot in life."

Very slowly, Slake reached over and brushed his knuckle over Raze's personal glyph on his neck. A burst of electric pleasure exploded from the thin raised lines of the mark Raze had never been able to identify.

"Is that why your personal symbol is an ancient Lydian symbol for acceptance?"

Raze jerked his gaze back to Slake. "How do you know that?"

"My people make weapons for species of demons you probably have never heard of. One or two speak ancient Lydian, and they always demand that certain symbols be carved into the weapons they commission." Slake pulled his hand away, but the symbol kept pulsing pleasantly. "So? Are you an accepting person?"

Raze almost said yes. But would it be the truth? He'd accepted the fact that he would never be a normal Sem. He'd never be attracted to females, and he could never be with a male the way he wanted.

But that didn't mean he liked it. And the more time he spent with Slake, the less accepting of his situation he was becoming.

CHAPTER SEVEN

Slake and Raze lay in silence for a long time, long enough that Slake finally realized he wasn't going to get an answer to his question. He wanted to ask more about Raze's relationship with the succubus, partly to gain any information that would help him complete his assignment for Dire & Dyre. But it surprised him to realize that most of his curiosity had more to do with wanting to know how Raze would be affected by losing Fayle.

It sounded like Raze truly needed her. For his life. For his sanity.

Fuck.

Slake shouldn't care. He shouldn't. After being rejected for who he was by his family and the one male he'd loved, a male he'd had been weak enough to let back into his life three fucking times, he should have been immune to tender feelings.

But here he was, impressed by Raze's medical skills and in awe of his ability to care for complete strangers, let alone a succubus who was too jealous to let him be happy.

Slake definitely needed to shift the subject to something less . . . Fayle.

"Raze?"

Raze's response was a sleepy grunt.

"I'm guessing I was onto something at the hospital when I asked if your buddies know the truth about you?"

Swallowing, Raze kept looking at the ceiling, clearly reluctant to go there.

"You don't have to answer," Slake said, but Raze shook his head.

"Nah, it's okay. It's just weird to talk about it." He crossed his legs at the ankles, and the sheet lying over his hips shifted, revealing a glorious hint of that firm length Slake had loved with his mouth. "They don't know. I don't think they'd be assholes about it, but I couldn't deal with the pity, you know?"

Slake reached out and traced a swirly glyph on Raze's arm as it rested across his washboard abs, loving how the dark lines seemed to vibrate at his touch. "Pity that you're gay, or pity that you can't be with males the way you want to be?"

"The latter. Probably." He jerked his arm out from under Slake's touch and jammed his hand through his hair. Slake experienced an odd twinge of hurt at the abrupt withdrawal, and it pissed him off. He wasn't ready to let anyone get into his heart enough to hurt him. "Fuck. I don't know." He gave Slake a sidelong glance. "What about you? I've never even heard of your species. Are you considered . . . normal?"

Slake barked out a bitter laugh and settled against the pillows. "Not by a long shot." He clenched his fists as if he could fight back against the bastards in his community—in his own *family*—who had not only rejected him, but who had called for his execution. "They accepted me until I turned into something they couldn't understand: a male who was attracted to other males."

The worst part about it was that he'd actually tried to change. And as long as he faked finding females desirable, his family was okay with it. Because yep, lying about who you were was okay, but being honest . . . well, that'd get you dead.

"I guess I was lucky," Raze said, a hint of an impish smile on his perfect lips. "My family only had to accept that I was a demon."

Slake laughed. "I guess being gay would be the least of your parents' concerns."

"They never knew, but they wouldn't have cared. They loved me no matter what."

Something inside Slake ached for that kind of acceptance, and for a brief moment, he was tempted to tell Raze the whole story, the truth about what he used to be before he was a male who wanted other males. Would Raze understand the choice he'd made?

Gunther hadn't understood, and Slake had never gotten over the rejection. Oh, Gunther popped back into Slake's life every decade or so, begging for forgiveness, insisting that this time, it would be different. This time, he could love Slake for who he was on the outside *and* the inside.

It was bullshit. It was *always* bullshit.

But Raze . . . he seemed different. Open-minded. Compassionate. Patient. Hell, the guy put up with Fayle, and as far as Slake could tell, the wench was a controlling, intolerant user. The fact that Slake had gone through a life-changing transformation shouldn't be an issue.

Should it?

Inhaling deeply, as if doing so would infuse him with courage, he decided to go for it. If Raze hated him, taking Fayle to Dire & Dyre would be that much simpler. If Raze didn't hate him . . . well, he'd have some serious thinking to do.

"Ah . . . Raze?"

When Raze didn't reply, Slake looked over, only to find the guy sound asleep, and damn, he was adorable like that. He was so peaceful, his handsome face relaxed, as if he didn't have a care in the world.

Slake wasn't going to ruin that. Soon enough, Raze would wake, remember that Fayle was a bitch who wouldn't let him have a relationship, and that his friends had died in a horrible explosion.

It was time for Slake to go anyway, and maybe this was the universe's way of telling him that he shouldn't get more involved. Shouldn't reveal secrets best left buried.

Quietly, he showered and dressed . . . and Raze didn't move a muscle. Clearly, he was secure in his sense of safety, something Slake had never known. He always slept with one eye open and a hand on a weapon.

Even when he and Raze had fucked, he'd always known exactly where each of his weapons was and how fast he could get to them.

Feeling only slightly intrusive, he went through Raze's pants in search of his cell phone. Once he found it, he plugged in his own number and then typed out a note on the screen. Nothing special, just a simple, *Call Me.*

As he stuffed the phone back into the pocket where he'd found it, he hesitated. He was going to have to grab Fayle at some point, and that wasn't going to go well. Sure, he could do it so Raze would never know he was involved, but damn it, now that Slake knew how badly Raze needed her, he actually felt pricked by a shard of guilt.

Suck it the fuck up. Your damned soul *is on the line.*

And Raze's life might be on the line.

Cursing himself and his situation, he slipped out of the bedroom and stepped into the kitchen where, lo and behold, Fayle was sitting at the dining room table, idly stirring creamer into a cup of tea. She wore a blazingly bright tie-dyed tank top, but the glare she gave him was all black.

"Sneaking out?" she asked. And rather bitchily, he might add.

"I left a note and my number."

"Hmm." She locked her gaze with his. "I don't expect to see you again."

Oh, she'd be seeing him again. Soon. If he hadn't used the rope he'd procured specifically for apprehending her, he could take her right now.

The guilt pricked him again, but instead of dwelling on it, he moved toward her, slowly, gauging her reaction. Aside from a slight tightening in her jaw, she was as cool as the frost on an ice viper's belly.

"I don't expect you to have any say in that."

A sinister smile ruffled the corners of her mouth. "I won't let anyone hurt him."

"From what I can tell, you won't let anyone near enough for that to happen."

She stirred her tea faster, the spoon clinking angrily against the side of the cup. "He can't be with males, so it's pointless for him to try."

"Seems to me that you're the one hurting him if you can't even give him the chance for compromise."

She bolted from her chair to face him, but some of her fury was lost in their two feet of height difference. "You know nothing about me or him, you effing piece of offal." She pointed to the door. "You got what you wanted from him. Now go find someone else to screw."

"*Effing*? Screw? Seriously? You can't bring out the spicy language to go with your insult? That's like serving tacos without hot sauce. Or throwing a Super Bowl party without alcohol. Fucking criminal."

"I don't like to cuss," she ground out.

Well, now, that was unexpected. Demons tended to be pretty liberal with what humans considered coarse language. "I don't trust people who don't cuss."

"Why not?"

"Because people who don't cuss are silently judging you. Pulling a morally superior act, but it's just an act. You know they're thinking bad shit; they just won't say it."

"Maybe they're being polite."

"Or maybe they're not being sincere."

She sneered. "Fuck you."

"See? That's sincere." He brushed past her and headed to the front door. Before he left, he couldn't resist adding, "Tell Raze I'll see him later."

I'll see you too, Fayle.

CHAPTER EIGHT

Oh, damn . . . I'm going to come . . .

The words fell from Raze's lips in an incoherent rush as the orgasm took him. Slake's mouth was magic, sucking and licking, taking everything Raze had to give. As the climax waned, another slammed into him, followed by another, and another. Slake's hand dropped to knead Raze's balls with light pressure, coaxing every last drop and every last shiver of sensation from him.

Fuck, the guy was incredible. As the heady glow of really great sex warmed him, he became vaguely aware of a tingle of pulsing energy flowing through his *dermoire*, and he had the strangest desire to flip Slake over, lock hands and bodies, and . . . and what? Bond with him?

Male Seminus demons couldn't bond with other males. They could only take females to be their mates. So why the hell was his body reacting to—

A metallic clank made him jump. Another clank, this time accompanied by a hard, cold *snap* and pressure around his ankle, got his eyes open and the sexual fog cleared.

"Slake," he rasped. "What are you . . ." He blinked at the sight of Fayle straddling his thighs. Her glistening lips and his wet dick lying half-erect on his belly made it clear that he'd orgasmed, all right, but not with Slake.

"You were asleep for nearly fourteen hours," she said, and was it his sleep-soaked ears, or did she sound . . . sad? "I took care of you before—"

"Before we had a repeat of the other night?"

Her brows shot up in surprise at the challenge in his question. Hell, even he'd surprised himself. He was usually one to let things go in order to maintain the status quo, but something had changed, and he was no longer content with the way he and Fayle had been living.

No, not living. *Surviving.*

"She's keeping you from being happy."

Slake's words filled his ears as if he was still lying right there beside him, and wasn't it funny how, after knowing Raze for such a short time, he'd distilled his life with Fayle down to a single sentence.

"No," she said softly. "Before I leave."

"Leave?" Gods, he was sleep-muddled. Nothing was making sense.

Leaning forward, she cupped his cheek in one palm. "I told you it's time to move."

"Wait . . . what?" He levered into a sit, and frowned at what appeared to be a thick shackle around his ankle. And the shackle was connected to a heavy chain that he assumed was secured to something solid.

Instantly, Fayle leaped up, landing catlike on the floor before backing toward the door. A dark, terrible suspicion welled up as he tugged on the chain. As suspected, it was looped around the bright blue pillar near the bathroom.

"What the hell is going on, Fayle?" he growled. "Tell me. Right. Fucking. Now."

"I told you." The tremor in her voice gave him hope that she wasn't dead set on whatever course she'd laid out. "I'm leaving."

"And you thought you needed to chain me up to tell me that?"

She worried her lower lip for a moment before asking, "Will you go with me?"

"Fayle, let's talk about this. Release me, and we'll work this out."

She thrust her hair out of her face with a frustrated shove. "Thirst is destroyed. And Underworld General will be fine without you. I'll release you if you come with me. Say yes. We can go anywhere you want."

"You're blackmailing me?" Anger rolled in, fresh and hot. "I have to do what you want or you'll leave me here to die?" He yanked on the chain. "Fine. I'll go with you." He was lying, but right now, he was willing to say anything to get free.

"I'm sorry, Raze," she whispered. "But I don't believe you."

Damn her! "Why are you doing this?" he shouted. "After all we've been through together?"

She smiled sadly. "I'm a demon, Raze."

"So am I! And I'm not chaining people to any fucking posts!"

"You know as well as I do that some of us are more demon than others." There was an emotional hitch in her voice that he might have imagined, except that her eyes had filled with liquid. Good. At least she felt bad about what she was doing to him. "I love you, but I have to go."

"This is love?" He yanked on the chains again. "Don't do this. Please."

"I have to. Someone's after me." She held up his phone. "But don't worry, I've already left a message for your lover boy to come rescue you."

"Lover boy?"

She rolled her eyes. "Slake. Ask *him* why I have to leave. And don't tell me you forgot him already. You were moaning his name while I was sucking you off."

"Release me," he roared as he leaped off the bed. "Damn you, Fayle, you can't do this!"

Very gently, she placed the phone and a set of keys on a shelf near the door—well out of his reach. "I'll feel your need," she said. "If he doesn't come for you, I'll call the hospital before you die."

"How comforting," he snapped.

"I'm sorry."

With a roar, he lunged, but the chains held, and pain tore through his leg as he was yanked, hard, off his feet to land with a thud on the concrete floor. Fayle fled, and as he shoved angrily to his feet, he heard her hurry through the apartment. A moment later, the front door slammed shut.

He was alone. And if Slake didn't show up in the next twelve to sixteen hours, he was in a whole lot of trouble.

Anyone who knew Slake well would laugh at him right now. And after they were done laughing, they'd kill him for being such an idiot.

Standing outside the newest of Dire & Dyre's law office buildings, this one in Tokyo, he stared at the ornate glass doors and wondered if he should really do this. If he should let his budding feelings for Raze affect his assignment.

No, he knew the answer to that: he shouldn't. But for the first time in his life, guilt was eating at him. And the thing was, the guilt he could deal with. He could learn to ignore it and carry on with his work. But what he couldn't deal with was the bone-deep feeling that Raze was something special, and if Slake didn't explore a relationship with him, he'd regret it for the rest of his life.

Which might be very short if he went to Dyre with his idea.

He eyed the doors again, watching as a demon disguised as a middle-aged black woman ran out of the building as if she were being chased by monsters. Blood streamed from her nose, tears ran down her cheeks, and terror wafted off her in bitter, acrid waves that burned Slake's nostrils.

If Slake remembered right, she was one of the thirty-plus lawyers employed by Dire & Dyre Tokyo.

The boss must be having a really bad day.

Inhaling deeply, he strode into the building, and the moment the doors closed, all of the city noise from outside went silent. Instead, a horrific, tinny version of "It's a Small World" pumped into the lobby in a nonstop loop. Slake knew it was nonstop, because in all the years he'd been working here, he'd never, not once, heard any other music.

Dyre was fucking diabolical.

Slake approached the receptionist, a hyena shapeshifter with overprocessed blonde hair and a perpetual case of the Mondays. "Hey, Richelle—"

"Mr. Dyre is busy."

"I'm sure if you let me into his wing, his assistant can—"

"No can do." She tapped on her computer screen. "Says right here that he's indisposed for the rest of the day."

He smiled, but only because baring his teeth would be rude. "Just give me an elevator key card." He gestured to the north hallway, where, at the very end, was the elevator that took people directly to the very top of the building where Dyre's office took up the entire floor.

"Do you like your eyes?" she asked pleasantly. "Because I like mine, and Mr. Dyre said he'd remove them with his own teeth if I let anyone up there. So go fuck yourself, Mr. Slake."

"Wuss," he muttered, as he reached into his pocket for his phone. Damn it, he must have left it at home this morning. He'd been too busy tracking down more rope for Fayle to remember. Ah well, Plan B. He smiled at the receptionist again. "I need to borrow your phone."

"Mr. Dyre doesn't want to be bothered by phone calls, either."

"Is that what your little computer screen says?"

She batted her eyes at him. "No. I just don't like you."

Gods, he hated hyenas. Of all the shifters, they were the worst. Arrogant, cruel, and they loved to push buttons. Just, apparently, not phone-dialing buttons.

"Look," he said, lowering his voice as he leaned across the desk, getting in her personal space and filling it. "This is really important. It has to do with a job that Dyre is very invested in. So you either connect me with him right now, or I promise, your eyes are going to be the least of your concern."

He was lying, but he was good at it, and doubt filled the eyes in question, turning them murky green. A moment later, she wordlessly dialed Dyre's office and handed Slake the receiver.

Dyre answered on the fifth ring. "What?"

"Hey, boss, it's Slake."

"Why are you calling me from the lobby?"

Slake smiled at the receptionist, who glowered at him and concentrated on banging on her computer keyboard. "Because I don't have an appointment," he said. "Look, I have an idea. How about you give my assignment to someone else? Give me something more challenging."

"No."

Asshole. "Just listen. I've found her. I know where she is, so all someone needs to do is get her."

"Then why haven't you done it yet?"

Good question. But if he could talk Dyre into reassigning the mission, he could tell Raze what was going on, give him a fair shot at doing what he and Fayle had done so well for decades: hide.

"It's complicated—"

"I don't care," Dyre snapped. "And now your insolence has cost you. I'm cutting your time in half." Dyre's sinister laugh crackled in air that had gone so cold Slake could see his breath. "Three days, Slake. I want her in my office by the end of the third day, or I promise that I'll make every second of the rest of your life a living hell, and then the day you die, I'll spend every waking moment finding ways to make your soul scream. Do you understand?"

Yep. Slake understood very well. Understood that he was screwed. And as he handed the receiver back to the receptionist, her jaunty smirk said she knew it too.

CHAPTER NINE

Raze had only been in this kind of pain a handful of times before. It was something he'd hoped to never experience again, and he shouldn't have had to. His arrangement with Fayle since then should have been permanent. They were partners. Friends.

She'd betrayed him.

The knowledge added an emotional layer to the gut-wrenching physical agony ripping through him. His heart ached even as his insides cramped and his cock felt like someone was driving nails into it. Sexual need was an angry, writhing thing inside him, a beast trying to break out of his skin.

If it did, no female was safe.

He had enough presence of mind remaining to know that even if Slake showed up right now, he couldn't free him. In fact, he'd need to be restrained even more, or he'd hurt any female brought to him.

But what if Slake didn't come for him? What if no one did? Fayle could have lied about calling Underworld General to send help. Or something could have happened to her before she could make that call.

Misery speared him as if he'd been impaled through the groin, and he fell to his knees, trembling, panting, trying not to vomit. His cock throbbed, and for a blind moment, he almost palmed the bastard. But no, he jerked his hand away, remembering the time he'd been ambushed by half a dozen Nightlash demons. They'd dragged him to their lair and tossed him into a pit, where he'd languished for hours, his need for sex becoming more critical by the minute.

Just before he went delirious with agony, he'd tried to ease himself, and for a few heartbeats, the sensation of being stroked had relieved some of the pain. And then, as if his body had known he was trying to trick it, the pain roared back tenfold, until he'd sworn his testicles were being crushed and the skin was being peeled from his shaft.

Thankfully, he'd passed out.

But waking again had dumped him right back into the nightmare. Fayle had tracked him, and she'd brought a dozen hired thugs with her. They'd slaughtered the Nightlashes, and Fayle had leaped into the pit to save his life.

Raze didn't remember much of what happened after that, but it had taken Fayle two days to fully recover.

Slake, man, where are you?

Granted, it was stupid to hope that a guy he'd only known for a couple of days would swoop in to rescue him, but at this point, hope was all Raze had. He'd tried everything else. He'd rammed himself into the metal post, but the thing hadn't budged, let alone bent. He tried to break the chain by pulling on it and smashing it with several heavy, hard objects, like the bed post and the nightstand. He'd tried yelling for help. Jumping up and down on the floor. He'd even considered sawing off his foot, but the sharpest object he could find was the dull edge of a metal bracket in the bed frame, and there was no way the bracket would stand up to bone.

He was going to die here, wasn't he?

The muffled ring of his phone penetrated his morbid thoughts and the marrow-deep agony. It and the keys he assumed would unlock the shackle around his ankle had fallen under the dresser after he'd tried to use a blanket to knock them closer to him. Now there was no way he could get to them. Maybe whoever was calling would worry when he didn't answer the phone. Maybe they'd come over.

And maybe he was a fucking idiot.

No one was coming. He was running out of time, and the bitch of it was that in a matter of minutes, a half an hour at the most, he'd be so far gone that he wouldn't care.

As his muscles cramped so hard he felt the excruciating snap of his ribs cracking, it was time to admit that he was, essentially, gone already.

Slake's day just got shittier and shittier. As if things weren't bad enough, he couldn't find his phone. Atrox was supposed to be tracking Fayle's movements and uploading them into a handy-dandy merc app designed by the best demonic software developers on the planet. Slake was especially fond of the kidnap-planning function. Those silly demon geeks were good.

He slammed his truck's door shut hard enough to make the old Land Rover rock on its snow tires. The phone wasn't in there, and the weird thing was, he felt a split second of relief, because if he found the thing and Raze hadn't called, he'd be more disappointed than he cared to admit.

He went through his house next, tearing apart the tiny one-bedroom cabin until it looked like it had the day he'd moved in twenty years ago. He unpacked drawers, ripped up cushions, and practically destroyed his bed in an effort to find the stupid phone.

Then, as he reached down to pick up a couch cushion off the floor, a glint caught his eye. There it was, hiding under the TV stand.

Cursing himself to a thousand hells, he plugged the thing in and had to wait precious seconds for the dead battery to get enough of a charge for the phone to turn on. After what felt like days, he finally swiped out of the home screen, checked for messages, and his gut fluttered when he saw the number of notifications waiting for him.

There were several texts from Atrox. And one from Dyre that had come after the fun incident at the Tokyo office. Probably another threat.

And there . . . unholy shit, there was a voice message from Raze.

Hand shaking, he pressed the Play button, and his breath caught at the unexpected sound of Fayle's voice.

"This is Fayle, you vile oaf. I know you were sent to find me, and I know who hired you. So trust me when I say I'd rather disembowel myself with a toothbrush than call you for help, but . . . whatever, I don't owe you an explanation. Raze is chained in our apartment. He needs to be released before ten tonight or he'll die. So . . . yeah. Help him. Oh, and fuck off. I say that with *sincerity*."

What the hell? She'd chained him? Why? And wait—

He glanced at his watch, and his heart leaped into his throat. She said ten tonight. It was midnight, New York time. Fucking *midnight.*

He had to waste valuable time driving to the Harrowgate closest to his remote cabin, but once he arrived at the site two miles away, he hit the gate at a run and popped out near Thirst. In a burst of speed he didn't know he was even capable of, he sprinted past the charred remains of the club to the alley in the back, and practically flew up the flight of stairs.

The door to the apartment was unlocked, and the moment he stepped inside, he was struck by a wave of what he could only describe as erotic agony. It was as if the very air was charged with both sex and pain, and the craziest part of it was that even as he tore through the living room toward the bedroom, his dick got hard.

And then he came to a screeching halt at the sight of Raze.

He was writhing in agony on the floor, his skin gouged as if he'd been trying to rip it off. Blood streaked his leg from the cuff around his ankle, and between panting breaths, he was moaning.

"Oh shit," Slake whispered.

Raze's head snapped around to the doorway, and Slake's breath caught in his throat. Raze's eyes glowed an unholy crimson full of rage and pain. Teeth bared, Raze snarled and lunged, only to be yanked backward by the chain. And that erection . . . holy shit, the Sem must be in utter agony.

Slowly, Slake moved forward. "Easy," he murmured, keeping his voice low and soothing, the way he'd once coaxed an injured dog out of a drainage pipe near the side of a road. "I'm here to help." How, he had no idea.

Raze went down on his haunches in a defensive crouch, and a growl, sounding as if it had been mined from the deepest pits in hell, rattled his chest. He wrapped a trembling arm protectively around his belly, and something in Slake's chest squeezed.

"What do you need me to do?" The obvious answer was to get him a female, but no way was he going to subject anyone to this. Well, he'd toss Fayle at Raze in a heartbeat, but he was pretty sure he didn't have time to find her.

A secret, shameful part of him was glad, if only because he didn't relish the thought of seeing Raze fuck someone else. Raze was his. Maybe it was just temporary, and maybe it was wrong to think of him that way, but screw it. Slake had spent his entire life knowing what he wanted and who he wanted to be, and for the first time, he'd encountered someone who might accept that person.

So for now, Raze was his, and he wasn't going to let him die.

"Okay, buddy, here's the plan. I'm going to knock your ass out, and then I'm going to get you to Underworld General. They can help you." He hoped. Surely a hospital run by Seminus demons knew how to deal with one of their own kind.

Raze's only response was a shudder and a moan.

Bracing himself for a battle, Slake lunged at Raze, locking his arm around the guy's neck and throwing him to the ground. But shit, whatever Raze was going through seemed to have given him super strength, and in a quick series of mind-bogglingly agile moves, Raze had Slake pinned like a WWF loser. And not just a loser. Like an amateur who had been grabbed from the audience and thrown into the ring with a champion.

Raze clawed at Slake's pants, ripping the fly open so violently that buttons flew across the room and seams tore. Slake's cock, so hard he could hammer nails with it, popped free, ready for action.

Slake didn't even have time to think before Raze hauled him up and slammed him, face-first, onto the bed. Slake twisted, but Raze was faster, and in this state, he was stronger . . . impossibly strong. In seconds, he had Slake's pants yanked down around his knees.

Gods, the guy was so far gone, so desperate for sex, that the fact that Slake was male didn't matter. But ultimately, it *would* matter, wouldn't it? If Raze couldn't climax—

He heard the sound of Raze spitting, and he cranked his head around just enough to see him spreading moisture on his cock.

Slake held his breath, his mind frantic as he considered his options, because even though his erection throbbed like a sonofabitch and his body craved Raze with an intensity he'd never experienced, his instincts screamed at him to fight back. His hands were free, and he knew he could stop this. He'd have to hurt Raze to do it, but hey, it wasn't as if Slake hadn't hurt—or killed—before.

Raze looked up, meeting Slake's gaze, and for a moment, time stilled. Behind the rage and pain deep inside Raze's gold-flecked crimson eyes, there was recognition. A shadow of agony passed over his expression, and Slake's heart stopped.

Raze didn't want to do this. "No," Raze whispered, his voice a tormented rasp. "I . . . can't . . ." He stumbled back a step, doubled over, and screamed. Screamed as if he were being skinned alive.

He was going to let himself die.

The stark reality knocked Slake upside the head like a blow from a troll's meaty fist. Raze was a healer who would rather die than do harm. He wasn't like Slake. He wasn't like anyone Slake had ever met, and suddenly it wasn't enough to merely get Raze help. Slake wanted—*needed*—to give Raze something he'd never given anyone.

Total surrender.

For the first time in his life, Slake stopped fighting. This wasn't about him. It wasn't about a battle to be accepted for his choices. It was about giving someone else what they needed.

It was worth a try. *Anything* was worth a try.

"Come to me, Raze," he said. "Now."

There was no hesitation. Just a sudden weight, a sudden pressure against his ass, and then the fiery pain of being stretched. The pain yielded quickly to pleasure as Raze began to thrust. Desperately. Violently.

Raze's fingers dug into his skin, raking and gouging, but the agony only added to the mind-blowing wave of bliss crashing over Slake as Raze churned on top of him.

Slake's cock, pinched between his body and the mattress, didn't seem to notice the lack of attention. With every pump of Raze's hips, Slake felt as if he were being stroked. His erection pulsed and his balls tightened, and when Raze fell forward and bit into the curve between his neck and shoulder, Slake shouted in ecstasy.

He came hard, hot wetness spreading across his belly. Raze was still going, the fury of his passion scorching Slake's skin where they touched. Slake came again, so forcefully his vision flickered, and then Raze was roaring. For a second, Slake went cold, fearing Raze had reached the point of failure and pain, but then . . . then came the glorious sensation of being filled up.

Erotic pulses shot straight to his groin, and another orgasm tore him apart. Shattered his mind. His senses. Everything went offline except his pleasure receptors, which were firing on overdrive. Time became one massive climax, and just as he was about to beg for mercy, because surely his heart couldn't take any more, Raze stopped moving and collapsed on top of him.

The sexual storm was over. They'd both survived.

But what, really, did that mean?

CHAPTER TEN

Awareness came slowly to Raze, clawing its way up from out of the black pit it had been buried in. A body lay beneath him. A hard body. A panting, *heaving* body that had clearly been strong enough to survive the sexual onslaught that Raze could only remember in bits and pieces as his mind attempted to assemble the puzzle of events.

Something sticky coated his skin, and a metallic, smoky taste swirled around in his mouth. Blood? Why would there be blood?

He shifted, hissing at the pain in his joints and muscles. His cock slipped from the warmth that had been surrounding it, and he heard a groan. His? Or had the sound belonged to his bedmate?

And why couldn't he see?

He opened his eyes. And wow, what a difference that made. The dim light spilling into the bedroom from the kitchen was almost too much to bear, but when he turned his head, what he saw was definitely too much to bear.

The room was destroyed, there was blood everywhere, and beneath him, oh, holy hell . . . Slake.

"Oh fuck," he croaked. "Oh . . . *fuck*." He scrambled off Slake, only now realizing that they'd both been lying only half on the bed, their legs hanging over the side, knees on the floor. Raze's useless muscles made him clumsy and jerky as he hauled them both more fully onto the mattress and heaved Slake onto his side. Bruises and deep, bleeding gouges marked his skin, and Raze's mouth filled with bile at the sight of the savage bite mark in his shoulder. "Slake? What the fuck did I do? *Slake*?"

Slake's eyes opened, and Raze braced himself to see hatred and loathing in their gorgeous dark depths. Instead, there was only drowsy curiosity.

"Hey." Slake's voice was as destroyed as Raze's. "You okay?"

Raze's mouth fell open. "Am *I* okay? You're the one I . . ." He swallowed. Swallowed again. But nothing seemed to quell the nausea bubbling up from his stomach.

Propping himself up with one arm, Slake reached out to gently cup Raze's cheek. "I'm fine. Gods, I'm so fine. I made a mess of your sheets, though."

The sheets? Slake was joking about blood- and cum-soaked sheets? "Damn it, Slake, I attacked you! I—"

Slake sat up and gripped Raze's shoulders, getting right in his face. "Listen to me. You backed off. You were willing to suffer in order to spare me. I could have gotten away. I chose to stay. I chose it, Raze."

"But—"

"No. I knew what I was getting into." He paused, and Raze held his breath, afraid Slake was going to reveal something horrible. "Well, sort of. But then . . . damn, it just felt good. And you didn't seem to mind that I was male."

Closing his eyes, Raze shook his head, hoping to rattle some memories back into place. "That shouldn't have happened. I should have—" He broke off on a sharp inhale as the implications of what had occurred sank in.

He'd come. With a male.

A *male.*

It wasn't possible. Maybe this was a dream. Or maybe he was dead.

His mind spun, unable to process everything that had happened. All around him, the world went fuzzy and sounds became muted, as if he was being held underwater. He broke out in a cold sweat, and distantly, he heard Slake's voice, felt himself being shaken. What was going on? He heard himself mumble something about keys, and then all went black.

"Raze?" A spike of adrenaline made Slake's hands tremble as he took Raze by the shoulders and shook him. "Raze!"

Nothing.

Raze was passed out cold, and while his pulse was strong and his breathing steady, Slake was pretty sure that being this unresponsive after sex was a bad thing. Had Fayle hurt him? Had Slake? What if being with a male had caused permanent damage?

Icy terror filled Slake's chest cavity. This could be his fault. *All* of this could be his fault, right down to Fayle chaining him up out of jealousy or some crap.

Ignoring his aches and pains, he fumbled through his clothes for his phone and dialed *666 for Underworld General. A growly female voice answered. "Underworld General Hospital. How may I direct your call?"

"I need . . . shit, I don't know what I need."

"That's not much help, sir."

Right. Yeah. Okay. Maybe calling was stupid. He'd get Raze to the hospital himself. "Never mind."

He hung up, threw on his clothes, and found a set of keys beneath the dresser, exactly where Raze's nearly incoherent ramblings had said they'd be. After he unlocked the shackle around Raze's ankle, Slake wrapped him in a blanket and hauled his heavy ass to the Harrowgate. He swiped his finger over the hospital symbol on the wall, and an instant later, he was stepping out into the emergency department.

Immediately, two people wearing scrubs rushed over. One, a doctor he'd seen before, the one with blue streaks in her black hair and a name tag that said *Gem*, guided him to an empty exam room.

"What happened?" she asked as she gestured for Slake to lay Raze on a table.

"I think he needs a doctor who is a Seminus demon to deal with this."

She frowned, but she didn't pause as she checked his airway, breathing, and pulse. "Then this is species-related? Sex?"

"I think so."

"It's okay," she said with a firm nod. "My sister is mated to a Sem. I know more about them than I really want to." She knuckled Raze's sternum, but there was no response. Even Slake knew that was a bad sign. "What happened, exactly? Did you find him like this?"

"No." He watched her finish inspecting Raze's self-inflicted wounds and then cover his lower half with a sheet. "When I got to his place, he was crazed and violent. He needed sex."

She grabbed his wrist. "Did he get it, or is he . . ."

"He got it," Slake said, hoping he didn't have to go into detail. "But then he passed out."

"Where's the female?" Gem's gaze flickered to Raze's blood-streaked hands as she prepared an IV kit. "She can't be in good shape."

"Ah . . ." Slake had never been shy about sex, but this was seriously uncomfortable. Not only for himself, but he also didn't want to betray Raze's secret. "His partner is fine."

"Tell her it might still be a good idea to get checked out." The doctor pushed a button on the wall, but Slake had no idea what it was for. "Now, I need you to wait outside."

Slake hesitated. He was sure Raze was in good hands, and it wasn't as if Slake could do anything about his current condition, but still, the idea of leaving him like this . . . it bothered him. Raze was vulnerable right now, and Slake had the oddest desire to stand at his side like a guard dog.

"Is he going to be okay?" he asked, needing reassurance before he could leave.

Gem offered a comforting smile. "I'm calling in an expert, but I wouldn't worry too much. His color is good and his vitals are stable. Give the receptionist your information, and we'll get back with you when we can."

Reluctantly, Slake left Raze in the doctor's care, but he didn't stick around. Fayle had done this to Raze. She'd chained him and left him to suffer. Slake needed to finish the job he'd started, but now capturing her wasn't entirely about his soul. Now it was also about revenge.

Fayle had just made this very, very personal.

CHAPTER ELEVEN

According to Eidolon, Raze had been in a coma for three days. Three fucking days. As he stared at the doctor from his hospital bed, Raze blinked his blurry eyes. The last thing he remembered before waking a few minutes ago was having sex. With Slake.

His gut churned at the memory, but right now he had to concentrate on why he was a patient at Underworld General.

He searched his brain, hunting for anything that could jolt a memory, but all he had in his head was Slake. And . . . Fayle. Yes, now he remembered her chaining him up, telling him she was leaving. That happened after . . . after he and Slake went to the apartment following the explosion.

Suddenly, he jacked up in the bed and grabbed Eidolon's scrub top. "Thirst . . ." He swallowed, but it did nothing to get rid of the hoarseness in his voice. "Nate. Vladlena. Marsden. My friends . . . how many . . ."

Lexi. Gods, her death came roaring back, and he sagged against the pillows.

"Ten people died in the explosion," Eidolon said softly. "Eight were customers, two worked at Thirst. I don't know their names, but I can get them for you. Nate, Lena, and Marsden are fine."

Raze swallowed again. Hard. "I already know one of the names," he said, and then he needed to get off the subject, and fast. "How did I get here?"

"Your friend Slake brought you in when you lost consciousness."

Raze shook his head as if doing so would shake loose some memories. It didn't. "I passed out?"

Eidolon jammed his hand through his short, dark hair, his frustration evident in his brisk, jerky movements. "As far as we can tell, you went too long without sex, which caused internal damage. The damage should have healed quickly, but when I tried to repair it with my power, nothing happened. It was almost as if something was draining my healing energy. Nothing we did could counter it. We just had to wait and see what happened."

Wait and see. The most common and exasperating words in the medical world. He'd said them a million times to patients, and now he understood why they didn't always take those words well.

He patted himself down through the hospital gown dotted with Underworld General's caduceus, and everything seemed to be okay. He felt fine. Didn't even feel the distant need for sex.

And wait . . . while a Sem was recovering from injuries, the need for sex would go into a hibernation of sorts, but the moment they were well, the need should hit like a punch to the groin.

"If it's been three days, why am I not going mad with—"

Eidolon, obviously anticipating the question, gestured to a full syringe lying on the nearby instrument tray. "A few years ago I developed a drug for Wraith that would temporarily ease the symptoms. I injected you this morning after I determined you were healed enough for the need to set in. You probably have four to six hours at best before the need hits you."

Great. And then what? Did he go hunting for a female . . . or for Slake?

"I'm glad you woke up," Eidolon continued. "Your buddy is a little . . . tenacious. He called ten times a day, and I don't know how much longer he was going to be civil about our lack of a diagnosis." He reached for a backpack on the counter and tossed it to Raze. "He brought you some clothes this morning. He didn't want you to wake up and not have something of your own to wear."

Raze's hand froze as he reached for the pack. That was the most thoughtful thing anyone had done for him in a long time. Especially considering the fact that Raze had attacked him.

The thought took a slow slide from his brain to his gut, where the reality sat like a jagged piece of brimstone. He'd lost control and could have seriously hurt Slake. And what if the coma was a result of going against his Seminus DNA and having sex with a male instead of a female?

What should have been a happy discovery had just turned into a stinking pile of shit, and as he pulled a red Manchester United hoodie and a pair of jeans from the bag, he succumbed to the realization that he needed to come clean with Eidolon.

Which made him want to throw up that lump of brimstone.

Standing to put on the pair of jeans, he spit it out before he chickened out. "Something's going on, Doc."

Clearly sensing that this wasn't going to be a light and fluffy convo, Eidolon sank into one of the chairs next to the bed that had been Raze's home for three days. "Hit me."

Raze mirrored him, taking a seat on the bed. Then he just sat there. Looked around. Tapped his fingers on his thigh.

"Whatever it is, you can talk to me," Eidolon said. The guy could be a ballbuster, but he always knew how to put a person at ease too.

Finally, Raze blew out a breath. "I, uh . . ." *Just say it, man.* "I'm gay." There. He'd said it. Cringing inwardly, he watched Eidolon, who, to his credit, kept his surprise limited to cocking one black eyebrow.

"Given the fact that we have to orgasm with females, being gay must be difficult for you."

Raze hadn't thought Eidolon would react badly, but his measured response, utterly free of judgment, still stunned him. His respect for the doctor swelled more.

"It is," Raze admitted. "It's lonely."

Eidolon inclined his head in a slow nod. "So what does this have to do with your current situation?"

"I'm not sure. Something happened. When I was all raged out. It was weird. Good, but weird."

"You gotta give me more to go on." Eidolon kicked his legs out and crossed them at the ankles.

This was so damned uncomfortable to talk about. "I was . . . I was with a male. And I . . . there was no female, but I . . . I came."

This time, both of Eidolon's eyebrows popped up, and his head actually snapped back a little. After a moment of silence, he leaned forward again, propping his forearms on his knees. "Are you sure it was a male you were with? There are a lot of spells, tricks—"

"I'm sure."

The skepticism didn't completely drain from Eidolon's expression, but at least he didn't push. "What species is this male?"

"Duosos. I'd never heard of it until he told me."

"Interesting," Eidolon mused. "They're isolationists. Rare outside of their communities. So rare that I've never met one, and we've never treated one here."

Raze kept to himself the fact that Eidolon had, indeed, met one. "What do you know about them?"

"Not much, and what I 'know' is mostly rumor and speculation. But if you were able to have sex with a male of that species, then one of the rumors might be true." Reaching over, he swiped his laptop off the counter and tapped on the keyboard. He studied the screen for a moment, and then turned back to Raze. "According to Baradoc, who developed the Demonic Biological Classification system, Duosos demons are born female, and at some point in their lives, they can choose to morph into males."

Raze sat there, stunned. The pillow talk he'd shared with Slake came back to him, and the words he'd spoken took on new meaning.

"They accepted me until I turned into something they couldn't understand: a male who was attracted to other males."

Holy hell, he'd meant that literally. He'd actually turned *into* a male.

"If that's accurate," Eidolon said, "and there's no reason to doubt that it's not, then maybe our Seminus instincts get kind of... scrambled, for lack of a better word... in the presence of a male Duosos who used to be female." Eidolon's dark eyes lit up with excitement. There was nothing he liked more than a medical mystery. "Will you be seeing this male again?"

Eidolon might as well have punched him in the gut. Slake had saved his life and brought him to the hospital, but that didn't mean he planned to see Raze again. Not that Raze could blame him if he didn't. Not after what Raze had done to him.

The memory lingered, an uneasy combination of both regret and excitement that the one impossible thing Raze had wanted all his life, to be wholly with a male, had actually happened.

"I don't know."

"Well, if you do, tell him I'd love to talk to him."

By "talk," Raze figured Eidolon meant, "poke, prod, and take a whole lot of bio samples."

"I'll let him know."

The door swung open, and Dr. Shakvhan stepped inside. The tall, curvy succubus offered a thin smile. In all the time Raze had worked at Underworld General, he'd never seen her show warmth for anyone except a potential sex partner. Fortunately for her, the fact that she was a top-notch surgeon made up for her shitty bedside manner.

"I'm ready for the procedure," she said crisply, and Raze frowned.

"What procedure?"

Eidolon stood. "Remember I said something was odd with the way you were healing? When I consulted with Dr. Shakvhan, she said it sounded familiar. She's here to test you for a sexual tether."

"A what?"

Shakvhan moved like a serpent. One second she was near the door, and the next, she was pressing Raze's palm in hers. "This is going to hurt—"

He yelped as what felt like a thorn jammed into his hand. "What the hell?"

"Shh." The succubus hummed, and searing heat spread from his hand through his body, the intensity growing until he thought he was going to pass out again. Sweat coated his skin, and his heart thumped about a million beats a minute, and just as his vision began to blur, she released him. Blood dripped to the floor until Eidolon wrapped his hand in gauze.

"Just as I suspected," she said, with an arrogance only she could manage. "He's linked to a female."

"Linked?"

She looked at him like he was an idiot. "Somehow, you allowed a succubus to attach herself to you."

"That's not possible. I've only been with one, and she wouldn't . . ." Would she? Surely Fayle wouldn't have done something like that without his permission?

"Whatever," Shakvhan muttered. "But I'm telling you, a succubus formed some sort of bond with you, and it's draining you."

No. Raze refused to believe it. He must have spoken out loud, because Shakvhan huffed with impatience. "Has she ever been able to find you, like, out of the blue? Have you ever wanted to get away from her but kept being drawn back to her? Do you put up with things she does and you have no idea why?"

Raze's gut churned. He could answer yes to all of those things. This . . . tether . . . would explain a lot, in fact.

"How can he get rid of it?" Eidolon asked, sparing Raze the humiliation of replying.

Shakvhan shrugged. "He can kill her. That would sever the link. Or she can remove it herself if she's so inclined."

Still half-numb with disbelief that Fayle could have done this, Raze asked roughly, "And if I can't find her?"

"Then it sucks to be you."

Raze clenched his fists, thinking how lucky it was for Shakvhan that the hospital operated under an antiviolence spell. "How helpful," he ground out.

"It's possible," she said as she opened the door to leave, "that another bond could break it."

"Like our mating bond?" Eidolon asked. "If Raze went through the mating ritual, the bond he forms with another fe—ah, person—could sever the ties he has with the succubus who did this to him?"

"Maybe." Shakvhan shot Raze a curious look. "Either way, good luck."

Raze wasn't overly fond of the doctor, but right now, he'd take all the luck he could get.

Slake had been searching for Fayle for three days, and now, as his deadline was ticking down to the final hours, he'd finally caught a break.

Fayle had led him on a wild-goose chase through the bowels of Sheoul, where he'd gotten close once, in a brothel in the Spectral Abyss. But somehow she'd slipped away only minutes before he'd arrived.

The trail had gone cold for a day, and not even a meeting with a Transylvanian Seer had given him a new direction to take. Failing at that, he'd staked out an underworld pub to rattle some info out of an ugly horned demon who did regular business with Fayle's people.

Big. Fat. Bust.

But today his luck had taken a potentially soul-saving turn. Using a sample of hair he'd found in Fayle's bedroom, he'd paid a Charnel Apostle to perform a location spell.

The succubus was in Amsterdam.

Slake rummaged through his cabin to finish loading a backpack with rope, weapons, and a few spell-bombs that would magically seal rooms and render him, and anyone he touched, temporarily invisible. He glanced at his watch and cursed. He had three hours before Dyre's time limit was up.

As he strode toward the front door, his phone buzzed. Hoping it was Raze, he plucked it from his pocket. His heart gave a huge thump at the message on the screen.

It's Raze. I'm okay. Heading home in a couple of hours. Call me.

Screw calling. Slake needed to see him. To know he was truly okay.

But first, he had to catch Fayle. As he hefted his backpack over his shoulder, the instant, alarming sensation of being watched made the hair on the back of his neck stand up.

"Hello, Damonia."

Slake froze in the middle of his living room. Went as still as an angel strangled by its own halo, as the ancient Sheoulic saying went.

No one had called Slake by that name in decades, and only one person was brave enough to try.

But too bad for Gunther that "brave" was merely another word for foolish.

In one smooth motion, Slake drew a *sinisphere* from his pocket and pivoted around.

"*Dhru'ga.*" The whispered command launched the tiny ball at the vampire's blond head.

Gunther easily dodged the weapon . . . until it made a U-turn and punched through his shoulder. He yelped as blood sprayed from the hole that also ruined what was probably a very expensive leather jacket.

Slapping his hand over the puncture, Gunther rounded on Slake. "What the fuck?" he yelled, his English accent making him sound almost reasonable, even in his anger. "A bit unnecessary, don't you think?"

"'Unnecessary' would have been sending an entire swarm of *sinispheres* at you." Slake flexed his hand over his pocket and the remaining dozen lethal balls. "But don't think I wasn't tempted. Or that I'm still not." Fury jacked him up so much that he had to relax his jaw in order to continue. "I told you the last time I saw you that if you came back, I'd put a hole through you. You're lucky it wasn't your skull."

Gunther hissed, the pearly fangs that used to give Slake so much pleasure glistening. "You were *aiming* for my skull."

"And I'm a little embarrassed by the fact that I missed." Slake raked Gunther with his gaze, expecting to experience the flutter of attraction he always felt when Gun came crawling back. But this time, all he could do was make comparisons to Raze, and the vampire couldn't match up. Not anymore.

Gunther stood there, his black slacks neatly pressed, his silver button-down shirt so starched it would be afraid to wrinkle. He had always been an impeccable dresser, but then, he'd spent a thousand years accumulating wealth, knowledge, and taste.

"You could have killed me," Gunther said, sounding so put out that Slake almost laughed.

"Stop whining. And stop bleeding on my floor. I just had the hardwood refinished."

"See, that's why our relationship didn't work," Gunther said, rubbing the puncture in his shoulder. "You're an asshole."

"No," Slake corrected, "we didn't work because I'm not female, and you couldn't seem to keep your dick in your pants."

Gunther's pale-blue eyes flashed. "I've changed. I want you back."

Son of a bitch. Not this rerun again. "You say that every time."

"And every time, you fall for it," Gunther pointed out, still as arrogant as ever.

"Not this time."

"Uh-huh." Gunther's skeptical expression pissed Slake off. "And why not this time?"

An image of Raze flashed in his brain, but he quickly shoved it aside. Yes, the Seminus demon had sexed his way into Slake's mind, but more than that, he was tired of not being accepted for what he was. For who he was.

"Because you're never going to be okay with who I am."

"I fell in love with who you are."

Slake shook his head. "You fell in love with who I was on the outside."

"Damon," Gunther said, "if that were true, I wouldn't keep trying to be with you."

"I don't doubt that you loved me. That maybe you still do. But ultimately, the fact that I have a penis will chase you away again. It always does. I can't do that anymore."

Gunther took a step closer and spread his hands in a plea. "What if I promised I was okay with it? What if I swore I'd stay with you, no matter what?"

"You can't do that," Slake said. He'd been through this before, and it always ended in disaster. "You know you can't."

"For the sake of argument. Say it could happen. Would you take me back?"

That was something Slake had thought of more than once. And long ago, the answer would have been yes. But too much time had passed. Too much had happened. And after seeing how Raze was so dependent on Fayle and yet so miserable . . . Slake could never tie himself down to someone who couldn't commit a hundred percent.

He wanted a relationship. He wanted love. And yes, Gun had loved him, but not enough to truly get past the fact that Slake was one hundred percent male with no remnants of his past. Well, except the fact that he was still attracted to males, just as he'd been before the transformation.

"I'll never take you back, Gun. Get that through your thick skull. I've moved on."

Instantly, Gunther went taut and looked around, as if he expected the person Slake moved on with to come slinking out of the bedroom. "You've found someone else, haven't you?"

"You lost the right to ask that question when you banged a female werewolf in our bed." Weird how he wasn't angry about that anymore. He'd held on to that particular grudge for the last ten years, but now that Gunther was here, begging to come back into his life, it no longer mattered.

Gunther's upper lip curled, his fangs gleaming wetly against blood-red lips. "Does he know? Does he know the truth about you?"

"Fuck off."

"So that's a no." Gunther shoved past Slake and threw open the front door. "Good luck with that, then. This saint of yours might be less understanding of your choice than I was."

Slake watched Gunther go, a sick feeling settling in his gut. What if he was right?

His phone buzzed again, and with a harsh curse, he looked down. Abruptly, his heart skidded to a stop so hard his chest hurt.

The message, from Dyre, flashed on the screen like a lightning bolt, shocking Slake through the device. He yelped and dropped it, but the words, two hours early, were seared into his mind.

Time's up. Your soul is now mine.

CHAPTER TWELVE

Raze wasn't looking forward to walking into an empty apartment. He'd lived with Fayle for over thirty years, and it was going to be weird to be there without her.

It would be good to be there without her. He still couldn't believe she'd attached herself to him through a bond he hadn't known about. The violation sat in his gut like an oil spill, making him feel . . . dirty.

Had Raze meant nothing to her? They'd never had a romantic relationship, but he'd thought their friendship had been based on respect and mutual need. Apparently, he'd been wrong about the respect part.

And now, after so many years of relying on her for survival, he was going to have to do what every normal, unmated Seminus demon had to do and dedicate a large portion of his time to finding females to fulfill his needs.

He dreaded the idea. He was so tired of being forced into survival mode. Slake had made him feel alive for the first time since he'd gone through his transition so many years ago, and if Raze could truly be with the guy . . .

He shook his head as he climbed the stairs to his apartment, trying to clear it of thoughts he shouldn't be having. Of hopes he shouldn't be having. What if finding sexual release with Slake had been an anomaly that couldn't be repeated? What if Slake didn't want Raze?

Nope, he wasn't going to get his hopes up.

He reached his apartment, but as he dug in his pocket for the keys Slake had included with the clothes he'd brought to the hospital, he went on high alert. There was sound coming from inside.

And the door was unlocked.

Stepping to the side and putting his back against the wall, he pushed the door open slowly, and noise from the TV grew louder. His first thought was that Fayle had returned, but almost instantly, he did a turnaround on that. She would rather pluck out her own eyes than watch *The Bachelor*.

Assuming that no burglar would break in to watch a mind-numbing TV show, he stepped inside . . . and sucked in a startled breath. Gods, he'd forgotten how damned gorgeous Slake was, the way his dark hair framed his deeply tanned face and curled around ears Raze had traced with his tongue.

His hands got clammy and his heart started doing a crazy flip, and he wondered if this was what a crush felt like. Was this rush of excitement and anxiety normal when the person you most wanted to see in the world was right in front of you?

He stared for a moment, taking in the magnificent sight of Slake as he sat on the couch, his leather-clad legs sprawled out in front of him as if he didn't have a care in the world. But the dark shadows around his eyes and the grim set of his mouth told another story, and Raze's excitement turned to concern.

Slake's leather jacket creaked against the couch as he hit a button on the remote, muting some girl who was wailing about being cheated out of some highly desirable activity with the bachelor.

"I'm glad you're okay," Slake said quietly. That voice. Raze had missed that deep, confident rumble.

He shut the door behind him. "Thanks to you." An awkward silence stretched, until he finally added, "We need to talk."

"I know." Slake scrubbed his hand over his face. He looked exhausted. Pale. As if he was in pain. "What happened the other night? What happened to you?"

Raze's stomach churned at the memory of what he'd done. "I'm sorry, Slake. You didn't deserve—"

"Not that," Slake said, sounding like a military drill instructor. Raze might have taken exception to being spoken to like that if he hadn't found it so . . . sexy. "Don't apologize again for what happened between us. I'd do it again in a heartbeat." His tone softened now, but it was no less sexy. "I'm talking about afterward. Why did you lose consciousness? Was it because of me? Because you aren't supposed to be with males?"

Raze stared. Slake thought what happened was *his* fault? "No. I mean, Eidolon has a theory about that, but being with you shouldn't have caused me to go into a coma."

Slake glanced away but looked back up so fast Raze thought he might have imagined it. "What's the theory?"

Raze kicked off his boots and padded into the living room, but he didn't sit. He'd been in bed for three fucking days, and his body felt tight and wired, like he could run a triathlon and still have enough energy leftover to scale a mountain.

"Eidolon said that every member of your species is born female. Is that true?"

Slake went as rigid as the support beams in the apartment. He averted his gaze to stare at the TV as if hoping for advice from the current bachelor.

"Slake?"

Slake remained in his statue-like state, gazing at the TV with a faint hopelessness in his eyes that punched Raze in the heart. "Do you know my name?"

"Ah . . . I thought it was Slake."

"That's my last name. The one all my people use when they deal with outsiders. My first name is Damon." He inhaled. Exhaled. "It used to be Damonia."

Raze didn't realize he'd been holding his breath until his lungs started to burn. He let it out slowly, sensing this was a big deal to Slake. "Okay."

Slake cut him a look, as if he expected more of a reaction. Or a worse one. Criminy, what kind of people did he usually hang around with?

"Eidolon is right. Mostly," Slake said, almost tentatively. "Every once in a while, a Duosos is born male. He is celebrated and revered, believed to be kissed by the gods, and he's inducted into the ruling royal class. All of our leaders are males who were born that way."

"I'm guessing you . . . weren't born male?"

There was a long silence, but Raze wasn't going to push. He'd dealt with a lot of trauma during the years he'd worked at the hospital, and he knew it was always best to coax. It was safer to lure a hellhound into a trap than it was to push one in, as the saying went.

Finally, Slake said, "No. But it's complicated. Females are . . ."

Slake trailed off, unable to believe he was about to discuss his species's biggest secrets, and not because he'd held on to loyalty for his people . . . but because he hated thinking about them. Hated who his people were, hated how they lived, hated everything about them. He hadn't thought about his past in decades, and now he was about to blow the lid off years of shame, humiliation, and hatred.

But this was just the beginning of his confession. When he was done, Raze would probably hate him. Not that it mattered. He'd lost ownership to his soul, and even now he could feel it growing dark, as Dyre's influence began to infect it. He felt sick, as if he'd eaten something very, very wrong, and every now and then his organs seemed to twist together in an excruciating knot.

This could go on for days, and if he was one of the fortunate few, it could kill him.

But maybe Raze would do it first.

Raze stood a few feet away, the very model of patience. He was a good guy, a rarity in Slake's world, and suddenly it felt wrong to contaminate him with his presence.

"I should go," Slake said, but Raze moved to block his path before he could even stand.

"You came here for a reason. You're safe here. You can tell me about your people." Raze's voice was deep. Smooth. Encouraging.

Gods, how long had it been since anyone had spoken to him like that?

"Females are . . .?" Raze prompted, and Slake hesitated for a moment before he figured he had nothing left to lose and relented.

"Females are raised to give males pleasure and be breeders," he growled. His days as a female had been little more than a waiting game as he counted the days until he could choose to change his sex. "Somewhere between the age of twenty and thirty, females reach maturity and develop the Mark of Tiresias. At that point, we have a choice. Ignore the mark until it fades in about a year, or go on a long, dangerous journey into what loosely translates into the Plains of Carnage, drive a bone shard into our chests, and wake up male. That's assuming you wake up at all. About half don't."

"Damn." Raze whistled. "Life must really have sucked if you'd rather risk death than remain a female."

Actually, life hadn't sucked . . . yet. Females had a lot of freedom until they gained the mark. As Damonia, he'd been allowed to leave the community for short periods, to experience the outside world. Getting out into the normal demon and human worlds had been an eye-opening experience that showed him how backwards and cruel his people were.

It was also how he'd met Gunther.

Gunther had shown Damonia the beauty of mountains. The wonder of luxury ocean liners. The pleasure of sex. He'd treated Damonia like a queen.

But there had always been something missing. As a female, Slake had never felt overly feminine, had preferred sparring with weapons over spinning the wool of his people's sharp-fanged demon sheep. It was said that females who humans called tomboys fared the best during the transition, so when he—as a she—had gained the Mark of Tiresias, he hadn't hesitated to take the journey to the Plains of Carnage.

Well, he'd had one moment of doubt. He knew he'd lose Gunther. As a transitioned male, he'd be attracted to females. It had always been that way, and there was no reason to think he'd come out of his change any different. Besides, his relationship with Gunther would have been doomed anyway. No post-Mark of Tiresias female was ever allowed to leave the community.

Ever. Runaways were hunted down and executed in the public square.

"Slake?" Raze said softly, and he realized he'd been lost in the past. Which was a shitty place to be.

"Right." He clenched his teeth as a series of cramps threatened to make him double over, and he swore he could hear Dyre cackle. When it passed, he hurried on, hoping Raze hadn't noticed the slight pause. Or the fact that his hands were shaking. "Yeah, life kinda sucked.

My species is extremely nonsocial. The only contact we have with the outside world is when we trade goods."

"What kind of goods?" Raze frowned. "And are you okay? You look flushed."

"I'm fine," he said quickly. "To answer your question, the blood of post-Mark of Tiresias females can be used to create and enchant weapons to make them far more powerful than they would be otherwise. It's part of why Duosos are isolationists; inside the clan, females give their blood willingly. But if a female fell into the wrong hands . . ."

"Yeah, I see the problem. But obviously, they let males out."

He shook his head. "Males have a little more freedom. They can leave for business or supplies, but they have to live in the compound."

"You don't."

"That's because I burned down half the village and escaped."

"Subtle," Raze said, and Slake laughed. He loved how Raze's laid-back demeanor put him at ease.

"Yeah, subtle. But I had to get away, and I needed a distraction. Once I realized that my gender had changed but my sexual preference hadn't . . ." He shook his head, remembering how he'd been thrilled at first, because he'd still wanted Gunther. Unfortunately, the feeling hadn't been mutual. "I had to go."

The shift in Raze was subtle but tangible, a tension that bloomed between them. "Because you're gay?"

"It's a death sentence for my backwards-ass people. But so is leaving the clan." He'd been terrified, knowing he'd be on the run for the rest of his life, which he'd figured would be short. Duosos were not only weapons experts, but they were tenacious trackers, and once they found his trail, they'd stop at nothing to get their prey.

It was those particular qualities that had made him approach Dire & Dyre with a deal.

"Protect me from my people and I'll give you anything you want."

Gods, he'd been an idiot. Gunther had warned him not to sign a contract with Dire & Dyre, but their relationship had been on rocky ground, which had pushed Slake even more.

Because he'd been an idiot.

Raze's feet padded almost silently as he paced between two brightly colored support beams. "Why is leaving such a big deal?"

"Because Duosos is more than just what we call our race. Duosos is a religion. A way of life. It's political. Social. Every aspect of Duosos life is ruled by our belief system, from what we wear to what we eat and how we reproduce. The only way out is death. Unless you're lucky and happen to have royal blood in your veins." He paused. "Life would have gotten real bad if I'd remained a female. I didn't want to be treated like shit. Used. Abused. I figured that if I became a male, I could try to make some changes. But the fact that I wasn't . . . *normal* . . . screwed all of that."

He glanced over at the TV, where half a dozen women were frozen in various states of smiling at the bachelor. He wondered idly if anyone on the show was a demon. For some reason, his ability to see identifying auras only worked in person.

Raze appeared to consider what Slake had said. "Your laws and ways of life explain why there's very little information on your species. I don't suppose you'd be willing to talk to my boss at Underworld General."

"Eidolon?" Slake paused as he reached for the glass of ice water he'd helped himself to when he'd first arrived. "He doesn't want to dissect me or some shit, does he?"

Raze laughed. "He likes to add to the hospital's database of knowledge. Every shred of information helps, especially when it comes to rare species."

In Slake's world of chaos and death, such a logical and reasoned approach to life and the mysteries in it was so foreign that he could only sit there, dumbfounded for a second. Deep down, he waited for some sort of judgment or scorn or something from Raze, but the guy just watched him expectantly.

"Ah, okay. Sure." He eyed Raze. "You're taking this pretty well."

"No one should be judged solely by their species," Raze said with a shrug. "We have demons working at the hospital to help people when ninety-nine percent of their species brethren would rather be killing than healing."

"Listen to you, being all progressive." Another wave of pain rolled over him, but he tried not to think about it, instead concentrating on the wistful smile ruffling Raze's perfect lips.

"I grew up with very practical parents." Raze finally stopped pacing and propped himself against one of the support poles. "And I saw for myself how no one, not even animals, fit into molds. I once had a pet duck that roosted in trees with the chickens. Her mate slept at the base of the tree."

Slake tried to picture the city-dwelling medic in a country setting and drew a blank. "You had ducks and chickens?"

"My parents had a little farm. We had a few of just about every kind of animal there is. That's how I got interested in medicine. I used to tend to the animals' injuries and illnesses. That was before I got my healing power, but even then, my dad was shocked at how well the animals did under my care. And trust me, they watched me closely."

"Why?"

"Because by then they knew I was a demon." He said it so casually, as if humans raising demon children was a completely ordinary experience. It did, however, explain why Raze was so different from any other demon Slake had met. "They loved me, but they were realists." He smirked. "They didn't want to find me disemboweling the family pig with my teeth or something."

Slake studied Raze for a moment, his gaze drawn to the designs on his arm that glowed when he was helping a patient. "Why *do* you have a healing power? I mean, you said Sems have an innate ability, but why? You're a sex demon."

"All Sems have one of three different abilities, all with a primary purpose of seducing or impregnating females." Raze's voice deepened, as if talking about sex triggered his incubus instincts, and Slake's body responded, his temperature jacking up, his cock stirring. "Some of us can get inside a female's head and trick them into thinking something is real or not real, but that same power can be used to repair the mind. Wraith can do that. His brother Shade can use his ability to affect bodily functions. He can trigger ovulation, for example. But when used for medical purposes, he can slow or speed up the heart, increase dopamine production to alleviate pain, shit like that."

Huh. Slake had an innate ability to control certain weapons with his mind, but aside from killing scumbags who deserved to die, he couldn't think of anything positive that could come of his skill. "So what can you do?"

"Eidolon and I share the same gift," he said, his voice still pitched low and still having a devastating effect on Slake's libido. "Mature Sems who have gone through the *s'genesis* use it to ensure that their sperm fertilizes an egg, but until we reach that stage, we can use our ability to repair damaged tissue." His mouth quirked in a sexy half smile. "Of course, we can also use it to rip tissue apart. It's a handy weapon."

"I noticed," Slake said wryly, remembering the werewolf in the alley. "It was awesome."

Raze finally came around the coffee table and planted himself in the overstuffed green chair that matched precisely nothing in the room except a painted pole near Fayle's bedroom.

For a moment, a comfortable silence fell, but gradually, tension began to thicken the air between them. Slake had shared a secret that he'd never told anyone but Gunther, but there was still the matter of Fayle to discuss.

Raze deserved the truth. But just as he opened his mouth, Raze spoke.

"So what now?" Raze asked. "I've never . . ." He trailed off, took a deep breath, and started again. "I've never been in this situation before."

"What kind of situation?"

"One where I want someone." Raze's freckles stood out as his cheeks turned adorably red, but there was nothing innocent about the promise in his steady gaze. "For more than, you know . . . just sex."

Ah damn. Slake had never been one to get choked up, but the emotion and vulnerability in Rake's voice touched him.

And reminded him that he was a bastard who was about to crush Raze's world.

"I think," Slake said softly, "that before we go there, we need to talk about Fayle."

"Fayle?" Raze went instantly guarded, his eyes narrowing. "What about her?" he ground out. "She's gone. And if Eidolon is right, I don't need a female as long as I'm with you."

The thought of providing Raze with everything he needed made Slake shiver with desire. To be the one who kept him healthy and whole . . . he wanted that. Wanted it *bad*.

But that was just a fantasy. Even if they could get past Slake's involvement in her leaving, there was the fact that his soul was, even now, shriveling like jerky. If he survived what was known in some demonic circles as The Darkening, he could come out of it a different person. Every last drop of decency could be wrung from him. Raze deserved better than that.

Clenching his fists so hard his knuckles cracked, he wondered why he was stalling. Dragging this out wouldn't change anything, and he'd always jumped into things headfirst.

Just spit it out.

"Fayle took off because of me," he blurted.

Raze snorted. "Trust me, it wasn't you. She left because—" He went as still as the gargoyle statue staring at them from the bookcase on the far wall. "Wait. She said to ask you why she was leaving." An icy wariness glazed Raze's green eyes, and Slake felt his heart sink to his feet. He hated that he'd put it there, that he'd just crushed Rake's hope for some kind of future. "She said someone was after her." He leaned back in the chair, just a subtle shift of his body, but Slake sensed an emotional withdrawal, as if Raze had thrown up a wall and was waiting for Slake to attempt a breach. "What do you know about that? What have you been keeping from me?"

"I haven't been completely honest with you." He locked gazes with Raze, determined to not take the easy way out of this. He'd face what he'd done head-on. "Fayle was right. Someone was after her."

"Tell me it wasn't you," Raze ground out. "*Tell me.*"

He wanted to tell him that. Gods, he would give *anything* to tell him that. "I can't," Slake whispered. "Because it was me all along."

CHAPTER THIRTEEN

Raze could *not* have heard that right. No way. But as he sat across from Slake, wildly searching his expression for signs that he was screwing with him, the terrible truth hit him like a sucker punch.

It lurked right there in Slake's seductively dark eyes.

He sucked in a harsh breath and stared at Slake in disbelief. First Fayle, and now . . . this. Suddenly, it felt as if his world was crumbling. It hurt. Gods, it felt like his chest was cracking wide open and his heart had been struck by one of Slake's *sinispheres*.

"Tell me what the fuck you're talking about," he growled. "Right. Now."

Slake shoved to his feet and strode to the window, where he gazed out at the roof of the deli next door. "We didn't meet by accident," he said, and Raze felt a painful twisting in his gut. "I came to Thirst to find Fayle."

The twisting grew more fierce. "Why?"

Slake's shoulders rose and fell with each breath, and maybe it was Raze's imagination, but his breathing seemed labored. Pained. Good. "Remember when I said my job was to acquire things?"

Anger rose up, swift and hot. "So you're saying that when you came out to the alley that first night, and when you came to me at the hospital the next day . . . all of that was to get to Fayle? You seduced *me* to get to *her*?" When Slake said nothing, Raze snarled, "Look at me, damn you!"

"No." Slake wheeled around. "I mean, yes, but—"

"But what?" Rage turned his blood to steam as he burst to his feet. "You figured you'd get your prize and get laid at the same time?"

Memories pelted him, of all the times Fayle had begged him to move, but he'd ignored her. She'd finally felt the need to take drastic measures to get away, and all because of Slake. Oh, sure, she'd also lied to him about whatever this crazy bond was that she'd saddled him with, but right now, he didn't care about that. It was too much to think about, too much betrayal for one day. Plus, she wasn't here. Slake was, and he was going to take the full brunt of Raze's anger.

"*You son of a bitch.* She's gone because of you. I thought she'd betrayed me, but all along, it was *you*."

The next few seconds were a blur of fury and the sound of Raze's fist meeting Slake's jaw. Slake staggered backward, slamming into the Kermit-green post Fayle had painted. Actually, she'd painted them all, and wouldn't it be fitting for Slake to get his face introduced to every one of them.

Raze took another swing, but Slake dodged it and settled into a defensive stance in front of the TV.

"Raze, listen to me." He held up his hands in a nonthreatening gesture, as if that would placate Raze, but fuck that. The only thing that would placate Raze right now would be if the bastard bled more. "Yeah, I was a shit. But Fayle was lying to you too."

"Really." Raze moved closer, eager to get going on the more-bleeding thing.

"Yeah, really." Slake touched his mouth, came away with blood, which gave Raze a huge jolt of satisfaction. It was a start. "She's a succubus—"

"I know that," he ground out.

"But did you know her species is parasitic?" Slake backed up, but Raze matched him, step for step. "They attach themselves to a host to draw energy from them. I think she attached herself to you."

The red pole was next. Raze moved closer. "I know that already. And right now I don't give a shit. I thought you wanted me. I thought we had . . . something. I freaked out, thinking I'd hurt you the other night, when all along you were planning to take Fayle. Why? To where? Were you going to kill her?"

As angry as Raze was at Fayle, he didn't want her dead. She'd violated him in a way that was unforgivable, but he also understood that for a lot of demons, going against their nature was nearly impossible. Instincts were powerful things, and the more inherently evil the demon, the less likely it was that they could ignore their basest urges.

"Kill her?" Slake bared his teeth in a vicious smile. "I'd love to wring her neck for leaving you chained up like that. But no, I was instructed to bring her in alive and unharmed."

"And you were going to do it by seducing me and kidnapping her. Nice." He lunged, fisting Slake's jacket, and threw him against a pole. The red one. Blue was next. "Why?" He slammed him against the pole again, and Slake grunted. His dark eyes clouded over with pain, but Raze was too far gone with anger to question why a little roughing up would hurt Slake so much. "Tell me!"

Raze shook Slake hard, relishing the echo of Slake's body hitting metal, relishing the way sweat broke out on his skin. Raze had never been one to enjoy someone else's pain, but for the first time, it was as if the demon in him was truly emerging. As if he'd let go of the humanity his parents had instilled in him and was going full monster. Shame niggled at the back of his mind, but he ruthlessly shoved it away.

"*Tell me why*," he rasped in a voice so thick with anger and hate and hell that he barely recognized it as his own.

"Because," Slake said, his eyes going flat, as if a spark had been snuffed, "if I didn't do it, I'd lose my soul."

Through Raze's fog of fury he struggled to grasp what Slake had just said. "Your soul. You mean, figuratively?"

"Literally," he croaked.

"Explain." He tightened his grip on Slake's jacket, ready to put him through the window if this was yet another lie.

"I signed a contract when I started at Dire & Dyre." Slake swallowed, his throat muscles working hard. Raze had watched them work when Slake took his erection in his mouth, and Raze swore he'd never seen anything so erotic in his life. And now . . . now they were in a damned nightmare. "I had to complete a hundred assignments, and if I failed a single one, my soul would become property of the law firm." He took a deep, rattling breath, and Raze got a real bad feeling about what he was going to say next. "Fayle was my hundredth assignment."

Raze sucked air between clenched teeth and wondered if this situation could get any worse. "So you're saying you still need to haul her in."

"No. It's over." Slake sagged against the pole as if the last drop of energy had drained out of him. "I failed. As of an hour ago, my soul forfeited to the firm. So do what you want with me, Raze. It doesn't matter much anyway."

Oh . . . *oh, gods.* Slake's soul no longer belonged to him? Raze knew how it worked, that the soul continued to reside in the host's body until their death, when it would be compelled to go immediately to its new owner. The new owner could absorb it, devour it, torture it, sell it . . . there were about a million things a person could do with a soul, and not one of them was pleasant.

Hands trembling, Raze released Slake and stepped back, his mind as shaken as his hands. "Holy hell," he breathed. "I don't . . . I don't know what to say."

"I'm sorry." Slake didn't move, simply remained against the post, his shoulders slumped, his gaze downcast. "I should have come clean. I needed her, but then I got to know you, and . . . fuck. I tried to get out of it, Raze. I called my boss, asked for a new assignment. I didn't want to hurt you." He looked up, anger encroaching on the sorrow in his eyes. "But I still want to find her and make her pay for what she did to you."

For a long moment, Raze stood there, stunned by everything that had just happened, but nothing was more amazing than this big, strong male who cared enough about Raze to want to hunt down someone who had hurt him. Not since his parents were alive had Raze felt as if anyone would go to the mat for him.

Slake reached for him, and Raze closed his eyes, letting Slake's warm palm cup his cheek. "Please," Slake whispered. "Forgive me. I'm sorry."

He was sorry. For trying to save his soul. Raze reached up and covered Slake's hand with his. "I wish you'd said something earlier."

"I—" Slake broke off with a pained cry.

"Slake?" Raze grabbed for him, but Slake hit the floor like he'd been poleaxed. "Slake!"

Slake writhed on the floor, his face pale, his body twisting with the force of his agony. "Hurts," he gasped.

Raze kneeled on the floor and engaged his healing power. "What hurts? Slake, talk to me."

He gripped Slake's wrist and let his ability sift through Slake's body, but he couldn't find anything wrong. Well, anything beyond the damage Raze himself had caused. He repaired the lacerations and contusions, but he might as well have slapped a bandage on a decapitation because Slake didn't stop thrashing, and his skin went even whiter.

"My . . . soul." Slake spoke between panting breaths. "Dyre is . . . torturing me."

"He can do that?"

"He's a Soul Reaper." He moaned, clenching his teeth as another apparent wave of pain took him. "Very powerful."

Raze had never heard of anyone being able to affect a soul while it still resided in its host, but then, he wasn't exactly the most underworldly demon.

"What can I do?" Raze was desperate to help, but damn it, he didn't see how he could. Helplessness wracked him, and all he could do was sit there and watch the male he had fallen for writhe in misery.

"Nothing," Slake rasped. "*Fuck.*"

Refusing to believe that, Raze gathered Slake in his arms and held him, bracing Slake's violent spasms against his own body. Slake's skin went from icy to hot, from damp to dry, and the sounds he made . . . holy hell, it was heartbreaking. It seemed to go on forever, but finally, Slake quieted and the storm passed. Gently, Raze eased Slake to the floor and fetched a soda from the fridge, thinking that right now, a little sugar would do him good.

By the time he got back to the living room, Slake had pulled himself onto the couch and was looking about a million times better, although his eyes were still bloodshot and he was far too pale for Raze's comfort.

"Here." Raze handed him the Coke, but Slake just held it on his lap, looking down at it as if it were the most precious thing he'd ever seen.

When he raised his gaze, the grief in his eyes tore Raze apart. "I'd better go. This is only going to get worse."

"How much worse?" When Slake didn't answer, Raze repeated the question.

"It could kill me," Slake said quietly.

Raze's heart skipped a beat. Two. Terror held the organ it its icy grip, and it wasn't until he summoned every drop of heated fury he had that his heart restarted and he could speak again.

"Bullshit," he snapped, and then he felt like a piece of shit for practically yelling at a guy who had already been knocked around. By life. By his boss. By Raze. "I'm sorry, Slake. But I won't let you go through this alone. And I sure as hell won't let you die."

Slake gave him a sad smile. "I don't think it's up to you."

Oh, no. This really was bullshit. Raze might not be able to heal him with his power, but he wasn't completely helpless. Not with his connections. He had resources at his disposal that the guy couldn't even begin to comprehend.

He shoved to his feet and held out his hand to Slake. "Come on. We're going to the hospital."

Slake shook his head. "You can't fix this with medicine. Let's face it. Unless you happen to be good friends with my boss, or better yet, Satan, I'm fucked."

No, Slake wasn't fucked. But if Raze could pull this off, he could also arrange a very thorough fucking.

Later. Right now . . . they had a soul to save.

CHAPTER FOURTEEN

"Okay, so . . . why are we at Underworld General Clinic?" Slake walked alongside Raze as they traversed the winding clinic halls that had been hidden within London's Tube network. He'd never been here before, but he figured it was as good a place as any to be if he had another attack of soul-agony.

Dyre was such an asshole.

"We're here because I called in a favor," Raze said, sounding unreasonably chipper for someone who was walking alongside a doomed guy.

Instantly suspicious, Slake narrowed his eyes at Raze as they turned a corner. "What kind of favor?"

Raze greeted a scrubs-clad horned demon who walked past them on hooved feet before turning to Slake. "Blaspheme, one of the doctors who run the clinic, is mated to the King of Hell. He might be able to do something about your soul problem."

Slake laughed, but this situation was so not funny. "Okay, sure. I'll bite. Satan's mate is a doctor."

"Satan's gone." Raze slowed as they approached the open door to an exam room. "A Shadow Angel named Revenant kicked his ass and then took over Sheoul."

Slake stopped in the middle of the hall and gave him a flat stare. Raze was serious. At least, *he* believed what he was saying. Maybe the coma had knocked something loose in his head.

"You're trying to tell me that Satan is not only real, but he's dead." Slake tried not to sound too much like a disbelieving dick, but come on. "And you know this . . . how?"

"Long story, but the short of it is that Satan is real." Raze gestured for Slake to enter the room. He was still wearing the clothes Slake had taken to the hospital for him, and he had to admit that the Sem filled out the jeans even better than he'd imagined. "But he isn't dead. He's imprisoned for a thousand years." He entered the room behind Slake, as at home here as he was at the apartment. "That's why there's so much turmoil in Sheoul. Very few people know the truth. Hell, a large percentage of the demonic population are just like you. They think Satan himself is a myth, just like humans with God."

Actually, Slake hadn't believed in Satan or God for most of his life, either. It wasn't until he met a fallen angel that his beliefs had been tested. If fallen angels existed, then so did angels, which meant there must be a Heaven. And if there was a Heaven, maybe there was a god who created it. But still . . . the idea of Satan had been hard to swallow.

"Okay, let's say you're right. Satan got the boot and this guy . . . Relevant? Reverent?"

Raze laughed and closed the door behind them. "Revenant."

"Revenant." Slake folded his arms over his chest and played along even though he was half-tempted to call Eidolon to make sure Raze wasn't feeling some aftereffects of his three days in the hospital. "Okay, so Revenant runs Sheoul. You really think that a guy who is powerful enough to defeat *Satan* is going to peel his evil ass off his brimstone throne to come to a freaking medical clinic to help out some stranger? And even if he did, there's the whole, 'making a deal with the devil' thing to consider."

Raze's cocky smile made Slake go a little weak inside. Gods, he wanted to kiss him, right here, right now, but he still wasn't entirely sure where they stood in this relationship.

"I've heard his throne is made of bones," Raze said lightly, as if they weren't talking about Hell's fucking *overlord*, "not brimstone. And what choice do you have? Your soul is already forfeit to a bastard who will do who-knows-what with it."

"True, but Dyre runs a law firm. Granted, it's the most powerful in the world, but this *Shadow Angel* you claim to know runs Sheoul."

"You still sound skeptical."

"You think? Next you're going to tell me that the Grim Reaper, Santa Claus, and the Four Horsemen of the Apocalypse are real."

"Well," Raze began, still all cocky and shit, "as far as I know, Santa is bullshit, but the Grim Reaper is real. He goes by the name Azagoth. And the Horsemen stop by the hospital every once in a while. They're pretty cool. But they can be serious assholes if they don't like you. Never get on their bad sides."

Slake rolled his eyes. Raze was totally fucking with him. "Look, I know you want to help, but I don't know that this is—"

The door flew open, and a huge dude decked out in leather stalked inside, his long black hair whipping around shoulders so broad he barely fit through the doorway. Massive boots with sinister metal talons at the tips boomed like thunderclaps with each step, and Slake swore the room shrank.

"Raze," he said. "'Sup, buddy. Blaspheme said you wanted to talk to me." He glanced at the watch on his wrist. "Make it quick. I have a Nightlash uprising to squash." He smiled, possibly the most evil smile Slake had ever seen. "Literally. Damn, I love my job."

"Revenant." Raze gestured to Slake, who suddenly wanted to back up. To Scotland. "This is Slake."

The second Revenant focused his dark gaze on Slake, all doubt fled. This guy was the real deal. The power emanating from him made Slake's insides jangle. Holy shit. Or, more accurately, *un*holy shit.

"We need you to buy his soul," Raze continued. "You know, if you want to."

"Wait, what?" Slake asked, incredulous. "*That* was your plan?" Bad enough that Dyre held Slake's soul. What would Hell's overlord do with it?

And again, holy shit.

Revenant and Raze both ignored Slake. "Why would I do that?" Revenant asked.

"Satan used to buy souls," Raze said. "I was hoping you would too."

"Satan was a prick. I run things differently." He glanced over at Slake. "So why do you want to sell your soul to me?"

Raze replied before Slake could even open his stunned mouth. "Because he sold his soul to a Soul Reaper—"

"That was stupid."

"Yeah," Raze said, without missing a beat, "we agree on that. Anyway—"

"No, I mean, really stupid." Revenant leaned against the doorframe and divided his unnerving attention between Raze and Slake. "I mean, it just seems obvious to me. Don't sell your soul. Seriously. Who does that? What the fuck?"

Suitably chastised, Slake scrubbed his hand over his face. "Yeah. I know. Fucking dumb. I get it. I'm full of regret. But what I need now is—"

Revenant's deep voice made the entire room vibrate. "You need someone who outranks a Soul Reaper to claim your soul and negate the deal you made with him, and you're hoping I'll be more generous than this guy. Right?"

Aside from his annoying habit of breaking into sentences, Revenant seemed pretty together.

"That's apparently the hope, yes."

"Huh." Revenant materialized himself a bottle of tequila and took a swig. "You're taking quite the risk, given that I'm the King of Hell."

Raze cocked an eyebrow. "You're also an angel."

"So was Satan."

"Satan was a fallen angel."

Gods, this conversation was so surreal. Slake had a feeling that if he survived the night, he'd wake up tomorrow wondering if any of this had really happened.

"And you think my status as an angel makes a difference?" Revenant asked, but he sounded more amused than irritated, which might actually be a bad thing. "I was born and raised in Hell. Satan's blood runs through my veins. What makes you think Slake's soul would be safer with me than with the Soul Reaper?"

Slake glanced over at Raze. "He kind of has a point. Maybe this was a bad idea."

Laughing, Revenant clapped Slake on the back. "Man, you're gullible. Not that I don't enjoy tearing someone apart slowly from their toenails to the hair follicles on their head now and then, but I make it a rule to only do that to people who deserve it." He paused dramatically. "You don't deserve it, do you?"

"Ah, no." Well, maybe, but fuck if he was going to say that.

Revenant clapped his hands together with malevolent glee. "Then let's do this." A parchment appeared from out of nowhere, hanging in the air, with a quill pen dripping blood floating next to it. "Sign on the dotted line, and your soul is mine." He added an evil cackle for dramatic effect, which worked better than Slake would have liked, because he had one hell of a chill doing sprints up and down his spine.

"Raze?" Slake asked, needing one last nod of assurance, which Raze provided.

"It's okay," Raze said. "I promise."

Slake read the document, which was simple and straightforward. Revenant would own his soul and could use it as toilet paper if he so wished. And yep, it actually mentioned toilet paper.

Slake scrawled his signature on the page, and the quill and parchment disappeared. "Now what?"

"Now," Revenant said, "you're mine."

"You sure?" Slake patted himself down as if he could feel his soul with his hands. "I don't feel any different."

"Do you want to feel different?" Revenant asked. "Because if you like pain, I'm generous that way."

Slake had no doubt about that, but instead of saying as much, he offered a simple, "No, but thanks anyway."

"You betcha. And don't worry, you won't feel any side effects as long as your soul is mine." He waggled his brows. "Unless you piss me off." Revenant opened the exam room door. "Now, if you don't mind, I have an appointment with doctor who promised me a thorough examination before I put down the Nightlash rebellion."

He took off, but what he said gave Slake a great idea. At least, he hoped it was great. Raze had just given him a priceless gift, a new lease on life, because now he knew he wasn't going to suffer at some bastard's every whim.

Without giving himself a chance to overthink this, he locked the door, pivoted around to Raze, and pushed him up against the wall.

"What are you doing?" Raze asked, but he was already breathless, and with his incubus senses, he'd be able to scent Slake's desire. Yeah, he knew damned well what Slake was doing, but Slake played along anyway.

"I'm running tests." Slake grinned as he tore open Raze's pants and went to his knees. "We need to find out if the other night was a fluke."

Practically trembling with anticipation, he fisted Raze's cock and slid his hand up and down in a series of slow, lazy strokes. Raze was so hard Slake could feel his pulse hammering into his palm, matching the beat of Slake's heart.

Raze's voice went low and husky, vibrating through Slake in an erotic wave. "Smart."

"So you approve?"

"Oh hell yeah." Raze hissed as Slake took his erection in his mouth to capture the pearly drop of liquid sex that had formed at the tip. The spicy, bold tang of the aphrodisiac that was unique to Raze's species tingled on his tongue and spread down his throat. Within a few heartbeats, the sensation infused his entire body, and when Raze jammed his fingers through Slake's hair as he sucked him, he felt it all the way to his balls. "In fact," Raze breathed huskily, "I think we might need to run a lot of tests."

That, Slake decided, would be a very, *very* good idea.

CHAPTER FIFTEEN

It turned out that being able to orgasm with Slake wasn't a fluke. Raze and Slake tested the theory several times over the next twenty-four hours, with breaks only to eat and shower.

Then, at hour twenty-five, they got a call from Dr. Shakvhan. She'd arranged a spell to reveal the bond Fayle had saddled him with, and as a side effect, he could sense her. The feeling was vague, sort of like a buzz in his chest that got stronger when he was facing in the right direction.

They found her in Amsterdam, exactly where Slake said she'd be, and Raze was able to lead them both right to her door.

Raze wasn't sure why he was surprised that she had holed up in a rented flat near the red-light district, but maybe it was because he figured she'd have hidden herself somewhere a little less obvious. A succubus in Amsterdam's red-light district. How original.

Then again, it was almost so cliché it might have worked. Even Slake admitted he hadn't thought to look here until some Charnel Apostle helped him out.

As they knocked politely on the door of her flat, Slake fingered the dagger at his hip and muttered a few harsh words in a language Raze didn't know. "*Bauknein maltz. Naychitz*! And how fucking stupid does a succubus have to be to hide in sex central?"

Raze snorted. "You're just pissed that you didn't think to look for her here first."

Slake glared, but he knew Raze was right, so he just cursed some more. Raze loved that. Fayle would have stormed off and threatened to make him wait for sex. But Slake . . . just a couple of hours ago, as he'd covered Raze's body with his, he'd put his mouth to Raze's ear and sworn that Raze would never again have to worry about getting what he needed. Slake promised to be there for him anytime, anywhere.

Raze nearly groaned at the memory, and damn his cock, it was remembering as well. Only the sound of someone on the other side of the door disengaging the lock prevented him from pushing Slake up against the wall of this dreary apartment building and kissing him senseless.

The door swung open, and Fayle gasped, tried to slam the door shut, but Slake's size 14 boot blocked it. Menace rolled off him in waves and his hand flexed over his blade, but he let Raze be the one to advance on Fayle as she stared in disbelief, her eyes wide, her face as white as a cavern troll's ass.

"What are you doing here?" Her voice trembled, and Raze took a perverse pleasure in the fact that it was the first time he'd ever heard her sound less than confident. "How did you find me?"

"Funny thing," Raze growled as he stepped inside, forcing her backward. "See, I learned all about how your species attaches itself to a host in order to feed off their sexual energy. I didn't believe it when another succubus told me that I was a victim of exactly that, but it turns out that a simple reveal spell made it clear. I can actually feel the tether, which led us to you."

Her heart was beating so hard that Raze could actually hear it. Maybe it was part of the spell that gave him the ability to sense her, or maybe it was because she was truly terrified right now, but either way, it didn't matter. She was off-balance and cornered, and it was exactly where Raze wanted her.

"Raze, I— You weren't supposed to find out. As a sex demon, you had more energy to give than most, and—"

"*Shut up*," he snapped, not wanting to hear any of her lies or excuses. "You betrayed me." He jabbed a finger into her breastbone, forcing her back another step. "You violated me. After all our years together, you didn't feel like you could tell me the truth? What *is* the truth?"

She flung her hand out at Slake, who had closed the door and was blocking the exit. "Why don't you ask *him*, since he seems to know so much about me. Has he told you that he's some sort of merc or bounty hunter? That he got close to you to get to me?"

"Yeah, he did. And it didn't take him over thirty years to tell me the truth."

She hissed at Slake, and nasty claws sprouted from her fingertips. "You want the truth?" she screamed suddenly. "How about *this* truth? If you'd listened to me, if you'd just moved with me when I asked you to, I wouldn't have needed to blow up Thirst. I'd never—"

"You *what*?" Raze stared, unable to believe what he'd just heard. "What did you just say?"

"You heard me." Her chin came up stubbornly, and he searched her beautiful face, looking for something, anything, that even remotely resembled remorse. There was nothing. In fact, her dark eyes sparkled with an unholy pride.

Fury and the pain of betrayal turned his breath into searing whips of fire in his throat, and he had to clench his hands at his sides to keep from strangling her where she stood. "*Why*? Why would you do that?" His temple throbbed and his vision blurred, letting him know how close to violence he was. "You *killed* people, Fayle!"

"It was the only way to get you away from that damned job. Your jobs were the reason you didn't want to move, yes? And that Lexi bitch. Gods, she deserved to die."

Raze literally shook with rage. Fayle truly thought that what she'd done was justified. "Were you planning to blow up Underworld General too? Was that next on your agenda?"

She sniffed. "I hadn't gotten that far in planning. I was hoping you'd change your mind about moving after Thirst. I had to get away, Raze. My people are after me. They're the ones who sent *him*." If glares could kill, Slake would be a greasy stain right now.

Slake shot Raze an exasperated look. "Can I kill her now?"

Raze was tempted to do it himself. But he had questions, and before anyone stabbed her in her black heart, he wanted answers.

Still, he found himself wrapping his hand around her throat and lifting her hard into a wall. "What's going on, Fayle?" Letting his anger reign for the second time in as many days, Raze got in her face. "You told me you ran away from your people because you wanted freedom. That was thirty years ago. So why do they want you now?"

She clawed at his hands with her razor talons, but he ignored the pain and squeezed until she gasped, "They want me because the queen died." She sucked in a gulp of air. "I'm next in line."

He stared. "You're some sort of princess?"

"I'm *the* princess," she choked out, and he let up on the pressure. Just a little. Just enough so she could talk without fighting for oxygen. He'd cut off her oxygen later. "I just wanted to be normal. To latch on to a male like every other self-respecting succubus instead of ruling a kingdom and popping out litter upon litter of babies in a world with no color." She looked at him, but her gaze was distant, shadowed, lost in a place where Raze couldn't follow. "Did I tell you about my lands, Raze? Did I tell you that there is only black and gray, and even the air is the color of mist? But the human world is so vibrant, and when I found you in it, I knew I'd hit the jackpot." A wistful smile touched her lips, lips made to make men beg. Men *and* demons, Raze thought bitterly. "Very few of us are lucky enough to hook an incubus. All that sexual energy . . ." She shivered, the light in her eyes returning and growing heated, the way it did when she sensed sex nearby. "But now I'm on my way home. I'll take my place on the throne. I'm just here to charge up and enjoy one last fling in the human realm."

He hated that he actually understood her thinking, because all he'd wanted since he'd reached sexual maturity was to be normal. And not even a normal, heterosexual Seminus demon. To him, normal meant having a relationship with someone he could share a life *and* a bed with. Someone he could talk to. Someone who wanted him as badly as he wanted them.

Normal . . . was Slake.

Very slowly, he released Fayle, but if she thought he was done with her, she had a huge surprise coming. He glanced over at Slake, who gave him a nod of understanding and pulled out his phone.

"Were you planning to release me?" Raze asked, staying where he was, which was in her face.

A shamed blush swept across her cheeks. "What can I say? I love you as much as I can love anything, Raze, but I'm a demon."

"So am I, but I'm not—"

She cut him off with a wave of her hand. "I know, I know. You're not sucking anyone's energy. Fine. Whatever."

Before he knew what she was doing, she was kissing him, driving her tongue between his teeth as she hauled his body against hers. She hadn't kissed him like this since the very first time they were together, when she'd helped him through his transformation. He remembered everything as if it were happening now, felt the electric sizzle unique to her kiss.

An unholy, possessive growl vibrated the air. Instantly, Raze's body responded as if to a mating call. *Slake.*

Fayle broke off the kiss and stepped back, giving Raze a shaky smile. Slake, on the other hand, had closed half the distance between them, had drawn blades from the harnesses under his coat, and was staring at her with death in his eyes. Damn, that was hot.

"It's done," Fayle said, keeping one eye on Slake. "My ties to you are broken."

That wasn't the only thing broken here. He'd trusted her once, but she'd broken that. He'd cared about her once, but she'd broken that too. He'd thought the last thirty-plus years had been about mutual respect. She'd shattered that belief.

"Tell me," he said, "if your council has only started looking for you because your queen died, why did we constantly move? Your species isn't really nomadic, is it?"

She plucked a candy from the bowl on the counter and popped it into her mouth as if everything was fine now that she'd broken the bond between them.

"Oh, we're nomadic," she said, "but that's not why I insisted on moving every few years. My people were always looking for me. The search just didn't get serious until the queen died." She bit down on the candy with a hard crunch. "Now, unless you're here to kill me, there's a red-light district that's just ripe with sexual energy to harvest. So go away."

"Oh babe," Slake said, his voice scraping gravel, "you're the one who is going away."

In a move so fast Raze didn't see it until it was over, Slake launched a dart that struck Fayle in the throat, penetrating so deep that blood spurted all over the pockmarked tile.

"What the fuck," she screeched, clutching at her throat even as her claws extended like a tiger's and her body began to swell and morph.

"Hurry!" Raze yelled at Slake. He tackled Fayle, taking her down to the floor as Slake wrapped her ankles with rope he swore would contain a succubus of her species.

Fayle swiped at Raze, catching him in the jaw, and pain seared him from the chin to his scalp.

Growling like a werebear awakened from hibernation, Slake snared her wrists and hogtied her, facedown on the cheap floor rug. Her muffled curses followed them as they both stood and looked down at their handiwork.

"You made the call?" Raze confirmed.

"Yup. Justice Dealers should be here any minute."

Excellent. Justice Dealers were the police of the demon world, and nothing gave them bigger hard-ons than tossing a royal into their jails. Raze was going to make sure Fayle paid for what she'd done to Thirst. And he'd enjoy every minute of it.

Slake turned to him, and abruptly, his humor turned to concern. "You're injured." Reaching out, he gently smoothed his thumb along Raze's jaw, and Raze sighed with pleasure that outweighed any of the pain Fayle had dealt him tonight.

"I'm okay," he said. "I think I'll always be okay now."

Slake grinned. "In that case, I'd say it's time I deal with *my* Fayle."

"Do you need me there?"

"Nope." Slake drew Raze hard against him. "Meet me back at your place. And I want you naked when I get there."

There was only one answer to that.

Duh.

For the first time in his life, Slake walked into Dire & Dyre's New York headquarters without an ounce of trepidation.

He was prepared for a battle to get onto the elevator, but surprisingly, the entrance receptionist sent him to the top floor without an argument. So far, so good.

When he stepped out of the elevator and into the plush offices that belonged to the Big Boss, Dyre's goat-horned assistant stopped him. Not unexpected.

"You'll have to wait. Mr. Dyre is—"

"Bite me." Slake shoved past her and slammed into Dyre's office.

Dyre looked up, but if he was annoyed at the intrusion, it didn't show. "Slake. What a surprise." He grinned, flashing sharp teeth. "A surprise that you aren't puking out your insides from the pain of losing your soul."

The jackass. "Yeah, well, how about another surprise?" He moved to the desk, planted his fists on the shiny oak top, and leaned in. "I. Quit." As an afterthought, he added, "Asshole."

Dyre's black eyes rolled like oily marbles in his head. "You can't quit. I own you."

"If you're talking about my soul, well, even if that were true, you couldn't stop me from quitting. My body is still mine, no matter who owns my soul."

The marbles in Dyre's eye sockets became ringed with red. Dyre had a short temper, and his inner demon loved to come out to play. It was probably time to de-escalate the situation. But only a little. Slake needed the guy to be agitated for what he had planned.

"I will kill you and reap your soul long before I allow you to quit."

What a dick. "You realize that when your employees are terrified of you, they won't go that extra mile, right?"

"They will if they like their skin." Dyre grinned wider, and Slake swore the number of teeth in his mouth multiplied. They'd also grown sharper. "Or their souls."

"Yeah, about that—"

A silver flash lit up the room, and suddenly Revenant was standing there, his massive black wings, shot through with silver and gold, arched high above his back. If Slake hadn't met the guy before, he'd be pissing himself. As it was, he still took a step back so he didn't get brained by the careless flap of a wing.

"So," Revenant said, his voice rumbling with such force that the expensive trinkets on the shelves rattled, "it turns out that when you own a soul, you get notified when there's danger." Revenant scowled at Dyre. "What were you doing to him?"

Dyre shoved to his feet. "Who the fuck are you?"

Revenant gave Slake a withering look of disappointment. "You really gave this douche bag your soul?"

Abruptly, Dyre's skin turned black as night and horns jutted from his skull, which began to elongate as his body doubled in size. Very slowly, Slake reached under his jacket for his bloodblade, a Duosos weapon only a male of his species could wield.

"You dare to insult me?" Dyre roared. "Do you have any idea who I am? *What* I am?"

A smile so cold that it dropped the temperature in the room curved Revenant's lips. "Do you honestly think I care?"

Every dangerous object in the room activated at once, all of them aimed at Revenant. In a blur of motion, he was pelted by various blunt instruments, struck by rays of melting heat, and impaled by sharp objects. But when it was over, he merely *tsked*, and everything went back to normal. His clothes stopped smoking, the blood was gone, and there was nothing pointy sticking out of him.

Dyre's black skin went ashen. "What the—"

Revenant lifted Dyre off his feet. And as far as Slake could tell, Rev was using the Force, because the guy hadn't moved a muscle.

"I did a little research on you after I talked to Slake. Seems you and Satan were pretty close. He let you do whatever you wanted with the souls you collected as long as you gave him all of your daughters. Is that right?"

Dyre stopped clawing at his throat long enough to croak, "Yes. I-I'll offer you the same deal."

The laughter that came from Revenant made Slake's blood freeze in his veins. "*You* will offer *me* a deal. Really? Because from where I'm standing . . . well, I'm standing. You, however, are floating in the air and slowly strangling. So let's try this again." He flung Dyre into a wall, shattering artwork, pictures, and Dyre's prized, framed awards and certificates. As the guy scrambled to his feet, Revenant advanced on him. "Here's the deal *I* will offer *you*. Return all the souls you haven't sold off or used for whatever vile purpose you use them for, and close your law firm."

"And what," Dyre ground out, "do I get in return?"

"You get to not die."

Dyre gaped. "Are you crazy? I can't give up my practice for nothing!" Dyre's hand slipped behind his back. Slake opened his mouth to warn Revenant, but there was no need.

Dyre exploded. Just . . . blew into a cloud of atomized red mist that settled around the office in a gruesome blanket of gore.

Revenant sighed. "I've had to do that a lot lately."

Ho-ly. Damn. "What," Slake muttered, "explode people?"

Revenant nodded. "Turns out that when you take over Hell, people aren't all, 'Hey, he banished Satan, the most evil being ever, so he must be a super-badass.' Nope, they're all, 'Hey, he must have gotten lucky, so let's see if we can take him down.'" Revenant shrugged. "Exploding people really gets a message across."

"I am *so* never pissing you off."

"Wise." A scroll materialized out of thin air, unrolled, and Slake recognized his signature. It was the deed to his soul. Revenant snapped his fingers, and the thing burst into confetti. "You're free."

"But . . . why?"

"Because I don't like being linked to anyone."

"Oh. Well, ah, thanks." He looked at the mess that used to be Dyre and felt sorry for the firm's janitorial crew. "So I got my soul back, but now I'm out of a job."

"Did you like your job?"

Slake shrugged. "No. But it paid the bills and kept my people from dragging me back to the compound and executing me."

"So why did you come here? To kill him and take his position?"

Slake held up the blade he'd had a white-knuckled grip on for the last few minutes. "I'm not a powerful enough demon to kill him, but I could have—"

"No way!" Revenant snatched the dagger out of Slake's hand like a kid who wanted another kid's candy. "This is a Duosos bloodblade. Do you know how rare they are?"

"Ah, yeah, I have an idea."

"You could have infused the blade with Dyre's blood and been immune to any move he made against you for a year."

"That was the plan," Slake muttered.

As Revenant said, bloodblades were rare, made even more so by the fact that each one could be used only once. Slake had planned to neutralize Dyre, and then he'd use the year to gather Dire & Dyre's scumbag clients for the Justice Dealers. Working with the Dealers to capture Fayle had been eye-opening and exhilarating, and he figured he'd get a kick out of using his skills for good for once.

Revenant flipped the dagger into the air and caught it between his thumb and forefinger. "Come work for me."

"What?" Slake gaped. "Are you serious? I just got out from under the thumb of one powerful psycho . . . er, I mean—"

"Stop with the flattery." Revenant held up his hand. "I get it. I used to be Satan's whipping boy, and it sucks to work for some evil jackass who is fucking insane and can end you with a mere thought." He folded his wings behind his back, and a heartbeat later, they disappeared. Must be cool to have wings. "But here's the deal. I'm the new King of Hell, which means people either suck up to me because they want something, or they think I'm going to explode them, or they want to kill me. I don't have anyone around me I can trust. You seem to be good at your job, and while I held your soul, I got a feel for who you are. I could use you on my payroll."

Slake's mouth went as dry as the sand in the Blighted Desert. "I appreciate the offer—"

"But?"

Slake really wished the guy would stop doing that. "But I won't kill anyone who doesn't deserve it. I won't seduce anyone. I won't—"

"Yeah, yeah," Revenant droned. "You won't compromise your morals or do anything that'll piss off your mate. Fine. If you object to a job, you can discuss it with me. I'm not completely unreasonable." He appeared to reconsider that. "My mate might disagree."

Revenant was one weird dude. But Slake liked him. In any case, he could be employed by a lot worse than the King of Hell. "You really know how to sell a job," Slake said, maybe a little sarcastically. "I'm in."

"Good. But I do have one requirement." Revenant's expression went grim and serious, and Slake had a feeling that whatever he was going to say was of lethal importance to him. "Never lie to me. Ever. And if I lay down a law, it is to be followed to the letter. Do you understand?"

"I understand."

Revenant held out his hand. "Then welcome aboard."

Man, Raze was never going to believe this.

CHAPTER SIXTEEN

Raze loved the forest. The trees. The wildlife. The peace.

And now, six months after Raze said good-bye to his old life, he was moving into his new one.

Which meant moving in with Slake.

Giving up the apartment had been easy, but he'd miss seeing Thirst every day. He wouldn't be away long, though. The new construction was almost finished, and he figured he'd be back to work there within the next month or so. In the meantime, he'd picked up extra hours at the hospital to keep himself busy while Slake was helping Revenant rule Sheoul.

And talk about a full-time job. Revenant always made sure Slake could get to Raze when needed, but Slake definitely kept busy. Today, however, they were both off work, and they planned to make a relaxing day of it.

"Breakfast?" Slake's gravelly morning voice went straight to Raze's groin. He looked up from his chair on the patio where he'd been sitting in the morning sunshine and listening to the gurgling rush of the creek a few yards away.

"Did you make some?"

Slake stumbled outside in nothing but boxer shorts, his sleep-mussed hair giving him a boyishly appealing charm. "I was hoping you did."

"Asshole," Raze said, hiding his smile in his coffee mug. His insult earned him a lingering kiss and a light but promising stroke of Slake's hand over Raze's rapidly swelling cock.

But Slake was a fucking tease. Grinning wickedly, he plopped into the chair across from Raze and sprawled in the sunshine, not a care in the world. He'd changed a lot in the last few months, losing the guarded wariness he'd worn like a suit of armor when they'd first met, and finally letting himself laugh. And play. And trust.

"Revenant said I can have a week off." Slake raised his face to the cloudless blue sky, a smile curving lips that could make Raze beg. "Can you get some vacation time?"

Shifting to give his erection more room in his shorts, Raze sipped his coffee. "Sure. Why?"

Slake shrugged. "I've never been on a vacation with anyone. You know, sun, sand, the ocean. I figure we can go somewhere exotic. And then hole up in our room and—"

"Fuck our brains out?"

Slake's eyes darkened, and Raze's cock got harder. He didn't need sex for another six hours or so, but he wanted it, and that was something completely new. Well, new since he'd met Slake.

"I was thinking . . . maybe we could try that mating thing you keep talking about it."

Raze choked on his coffee. Just a little. But still. "Mating? You want to mate with me? Like, I'll be tied to you until one of us dies? That mating?"

Slake braced his elbows on his spread legs and leaned forward even as his voice lowered to an intimate purr. "When you put it that way . . . yeah."

A flurry of emotions washed over Raze, but he couldn't grab on to one. It was as if he was happy and panicked and angry that it might not be possible, all at once.

Bonding. Damn. It was a mating ritual that, until now, had only been something Seminus demons did with females. Would it even be possible with a male? With a female, the bond was pretty much a one-way street, allowing the female to control the reins. She gained a *dermoire* that matched her mate's, but on the opposite arm, while the male . . . well, that's where the bond truly rested. A bonded male could never have sex with anyone else as long as his mate lived. To bond with someone was a major commitment. A *life* commitment, and given that his lifespan ran hundreds of years . . .

"Hey," Slake said quietly. "We don't have to. I know the thing with Fayle was fucked up, and if I were you, I wouldn't let the word *bond* into my vocabulary. But I was just thinking—"

"No, I want to," Raze blurted, because the hell if he was going to let this opportunity slip through his fingers. "I do. It's just that I don't know if it's possible between two males."

"We can have sex, and before you met me, that wasn't supposed to be possible, either. We won't know until we try."

True. But it was a huge step.

Beyond huge.

And it was a no-brainer.

Raze had been waiting all his life for Slake, and now that he had him, he wasn't letting him go.

He stood and held out his hand to the magnificent male who had given him so much. Slake's hand closed around his, and together they made their way to the bedroom. They peeled off their shorts, and in a rare moment of awkwardness, they faced each other, naked in more ways than one.

"How does this work?" Slake asked, his voice deep and eager, and Raze's body responded with a rush of endorphins that said this was right. Everything about this was right.

"I don't know . . ." Actually, Raze did know. His instincts were rising in him, telling him what to do next, and without thinking, he reached for the blade Slake always kept on the nightstand.

"Your eyes," Slake breathed. "They're pure gold. I know they get that way when you're turned on, but this . . . Wow."

Raze stepped into him so they were chest to chest, and with a desperation he couldn't explain, he took Slake's mouth, licking at the seam of his lips until Slake let him in.

As they fell to the bed, Raze slashed the sharp edge of the blade across his chest. The pain was sharp but fleeting, dulled by the anticipation of what was coming next.

"You need to drink," he murmured against Slake's mouth. "Now."

Slake didn't hesitate. The scent of his arousal drifted up to Raze, kicking his own arousal up a notch as Slake kissed his way down Raze's neck, lingering only to nip his collarbone and make Raze growl with pleasure. But the moment Slake's mouth closed on the cut he'd made, the pleasure became so intense that he didn't think he'd survive it.

"Raze," Slake whispered against his skin. "Damn, you taste . . . good." He dragged his tongue along the length of the cut as Raze reached for the lube.

"Now," Raze moaned. "I need to be inside you *now*. But you have to do it. You have to be willing."

Slake looked up, confused, but a heartbeat later, he was drizzling a cool stream of lube on Raze's hard cock with one hand and fondling his balls with the other. Sweet, sweet agony rippled upward from Raze's groin. As always, Slake's touch was magic. He intuitively knew what Raze wanted and how he wanted it, how hard, how fast, how deep, and Raze could only imagine that if the bonding worked, they'd be even more in sync. The possibilities were endless and almost incomprehensible.

Every muscle in Slake's arms rippled under his supple skin as he crawled up Raze's body, kissing and licking along every inch of the journey. His dark eyes glowed with need as he gazed down at Raze, and damned if Raze didn't swell with emotion. He loved Slake with every cell in his body, and if that wasn't good enough for a bond, he didn't know what was.

Slowly, gently, Slake eased back onto Raze's erection. Ecstasy engulfed Raze as Slake seated himself fully and began to move, his hot, tight ass clenching with every stroke.

Raze barely had the presence of mind to lift the dagger off the mattress. "You need to cut yourself. Right wrist. I have to drink."

If Raze thought Slake would balk, he'd been dead wrong. In a single, smooth motion, Slake slashed the blade across his wrist and held it to Raze's mouth.

Warm, silky blood dripped onto Raze's tongue, and holy shit, he might as well have plugged into an electrical socket, because his body began to spark and tingle. He'd become a live wire, connected to Slake in a way he couldn't have anticipated. Couldn't have even hoped for because he hadn't known such a feeling existed.

On the verge of orgasm, he twined his fingers with Slake's, Raze's right hand with Slake's left. As he drew on Slake's vein, a current cycled through them, and Raze felt everything Slake was feeling. There was affection, warmth, respect, love. They were connected in so many ways, and it was so . . . right.

"Raze," Slake gasped. "Aw, damn, I can . . . feel you." He rocked against Raze, his entire body turning into a storm of sex and passion that couldn't be contained.

Raze took a deep pull on Slake's wrist as ecstasy launched him over the edge. He threw his head back and arched into Slake, slamming him forward so hard he had to brace himself against the wall. Plaster rained down on Raze's head, but he barely noticed, too lost in the full-body orgasm that wouldn't end.

Distantly, he heard Slake shout as Raze pumped into him. Hot, wet splashes struck his chest, his neck, his chin. The musky scent of Slake's cum coated his skin and drove Raze to new heights.

He lost track of time and orgasms. Eventually, maybe a month later, if his exhaustion was any indication, he reached full awareness and found himself on top of Slake, their hot, damp skin plastering them together. At some point he'd flipped Slake onto his back, their hands linked, their mouths locked.

Slake was half-gone, his drowsy eyes barely cracked as he looked up at Raze. "I think," he breathed, "that I'm dead."

"I know I am," he groaned. Gods, his entire body felt like rubber, and yet, a new, strange energy infused him. *Slake*, he thought. The new energy was Slake. Raze could feel him everywhere. Inside. Outside. In his head.

Right now, Slake was happy. Content. As Raze gazed down at the best thing that ever happened to him, Slake smiled. "You're happy."

"We're bonded."

As if Slake's arm weighed half a ton, he hefted it up. "Holy shit," he breathed. "Look."

Raze struggled to focus his eyes, and when they finally went 20/20, he grinned. Black lines were beginning to appear on Slake's hand and spread up his arm, solidifying in a perfect copy of Raze's *dermoire.*

"It's amazing." Raze stared in awe. "Beautiful."

Slake reached out and brushed his finger over Raze's throat. His skin tingled under Slake's fingertip and spread like erotic hellfire around his neck. "It's happening," he murmured. "You're getting the mate rings. We just made history."

Raze would have laughed if he'd had the energy. "Eidolon is going to fucking come in his pants when I tell him. He loves anomalies."

"I love *you*."

Rolling to one side, Raze twined their fingers and brought Slake with him. They were messy and sweaty and needed to shower, but they could do that in a minute. Right now, all Raze wanted was to enjoy the one thing he never thought he could have. To say the one thing he never thought he'd say.

"I love you too."

Dear Reader,

Thank you for reading Larissa Ione's *Base Instincts*!

We know your time is precious and you have many, many entertainment options, so it means a lot that you've chosen to spend your time reading. We really hope you enjoyed it.

We'd be honored if you'd consider posting a review—good or bad—on sites like **Amazon, Barnes & Noble, Kobo, Goodreads, Twitter, Facebook, Tumblr,** and your blog or website. We'd also be honored if you told your friends and family about this book. Word of mouth is a book's lifeblood!

For more information on upcoming releases, author interviews, blog tours, contests, giveaways, and more, please sign up for our weekly, spam-free newsletter and visit us around the web:

Newsletter: tinyurl.com/RiptideSignup
Twitter: twitter.com/RiptideBooks
Facebook: facebook.com/RiptidePublishing
Goodreads: tinyurl.com/RiptideOnGoodreads
Tumblr: riptidepublishing.tumblr.com

Thank you so much for Reading the Rainbow!

RiptidePublishing.com

ACKNOWLEDGMENTS

I just want to send a quick thank-you to all my established readers who followed me to Raze and Slake's story. Thank you for your support and faith. You keep me going! And to all my new readers, thank you for giving me a shot. I hope you enjoyed your first foray into my Demonica world!

And a special thanks to Riptide Publishing, especially Sarah Frantz Lyons, for giving me a chance to expand my Demonica universe. I appreciate everything you've done to help make this book the best it can be!

ALSO BY LARISSA IONE

Demonica/Lords of Deliverance Series

Pleasure Unbound
Desire Unchained
Passion Unleashed
Ecstasy Unveiled
Sin Undone
Eternal Rider
Vampire Fight Club (part of the *Supernatural* anthology)
Immortal Rider
Lethal Rider
Rogue Rider
Reaver
Azagoth
Revenant
Hades

Moonbound Clan Vampires Series

Bound By Night
Chained By Night

Cowriting as Sydney Croft

Riding The Storm
Unleashing The Storm
Seduced By The Storm
Taming The Fire
Tempting The Fire
Taken By Fire
Three The Hard Way

ABOUT THE AUTHOR

Air Force veteran Larissa Ione traded in a career as a meteorologist to pursue her passion of writing. She has since published dozens of books, hit several bestseller lists, including the *New York Times* and *USA Today*, and has been nominated for a RITA award. She now spends her days in pajamas with her computer, strong coffee, and supernatural worlds. She believes in celebrating everything and would never be caught without a bottle of champagne chilling in the fridge . . . just in case. She currently lives in Wisconsin with her US Coast Guard husband, her teenage son, a rescue cat named Vegas, and her very own hellhound, a King Shepherd named Hexe.

You can find out more about Larissa and her works here:

Website: larissaIone.com

Facebook: facebook.com/OfficialLarissaIone

Twitter: twitter.com/LarissaIone

Pinterest: pinterest.com/LarissaIone